WHAT COLETTE DIDN'T KNOW

Hans Konrad, department manager in an insurance company falls in love with a stewardess on a flight to Seoul. Later he discovers she's French living in Paris. Hans regularly travels to Paris where the company has an office, so he arranges a date with Colette. The date sparks off a love affair, and only two months later Hans proposes marriage, which, after some consideration, Colette accepts. She moves to Frankfurt, where they get married. Back from their honeymoon in Crete, Hans finds a letter on his desk, which turns out to be his dismissal. Hans keeps it a secret from Colette and goes out every morning as if going to work. Hans and Colette keep in touch by mobile, but on December, 6th on her way home from work, Colette wants to phone Hans but finds her mobile doesn't work. She checks her notebook for the office number and dials from a telephone box. It's not Hans she hears, but a female voice telling her Mr Konrad is no longer with the company. On inquiry, Colette is told that he left the company last June.

By the same author:

Poems and Limericks

WHAT COLETTE DIDN'T KNOW

Mike Crowley was born in 1941 in Cork City. He lived in Dublin, Frankfurt, West Berlin, Perugia and Rome. Later he returned to Frankfurt, where he lives today.

Mike Crowley

WHAT

COLETTE

DIDN'T KNOW

© Copyright 2006 Mike Crowley.
All rights reserved. No part of this publication may be reproduced, stored in a retrieval system, or transmitted, in any form or by any means, electronic, mechanical, photocopying, recording, or otherwise, without the written prior permission of the author.

This novel is a work of fiction. Names, characters and incidents either are the product of the author's imagination or are used fictitiously. Any resemblance to actual persons, living or dead or events is entirely coincidental.

Note for Librarians: A cataloguing record for this book is available from Library and Archives Canada at www.collectionscanada.ca/amicus/index-e.html
ISBN 1-4251-0297-2

Printed in Victoria, BC, Canada. Printed on paper with minimum 30% recycled fibre. Trafford's print shop runs on "green energy" from solar, wind and other environmentally-friendly power sources.

Offices in Canada, USA, Ireland and UK

Book sales for North America and international:
Trafford Publishing, 6E–2333 Government St.,
Victoria, BC V8T 4P4 CANADA
phone 250 383 6864 (toll-free 1 888 232 4444)
fax 250 383 6804; email to orders@trafford.com
Book sales in Europe:
Trafford Publishing (UK) Limited, 9 Park End Street, 2nd Floor
Oxford, UK OX1 1HH UNITED KINGDOM
phone 44 (0)1865 722 113 (local rate 0845 230 9601)
facsimile 44 (0)1865 722 868; info.uk@trafford.com
Order online at:
trafford.com/06-2054

10 9 8 7 6 5 4 3

ACKNOWLEDGEMENT

Thanks to imagination without which there could be no fiction.

"Wonderful are the works of a wheelbarrow."

(a favourite saying of my grandfather, and the only person I ever heard use the saying.)

WHAT COLETTE DIDN'T KNOW

Chapter 1

You'll have time now, she shouted, you'll have plenty of time now for all that writing you're bragging about.

Colette slammed the door behind her and went off to work. The chilly nip in the early morning air hit her bubbling anger like a shock therapy and she pulled the collar of her newly bought winter coat closer round her neck as she hurried to catch the tram. The streets were deserted except for a few cars speeding by and a few people waiting for the tram. When the tram came and she climbed onto it, a wave of heat mingled with a stink of foul

Mike Crowley

air encircled her nose. She found a vacant seat to herself and as the tram moved off an empty beer bottle rolled across the floor landing with a bump against her shoe. At first she wanted to give it a kick and send it spinning down the aisle, but then she was afraid it might crash against something and smash. As the tram swung into Konrad Adenhauer Street the bottle rolled away. Bastard! she exclaimed in a hushed voice. This didn't refer to the bottle, but to Hans. She hadn't reckoned with anything like the night before. But again it wasn't so much the thing itself, though now, of course she could no longer trust him. No, it was the fact that she herself could have been so blind as not to have noticed anything strange in his behaviour. This was the distressing thing about it.

Hans, still in pyjamas and dressing-gown remained seated at the breakfast table. He lit a cigarette and sat wondering how to put in the day as he watched the smoke that trickled from his nose float in the air and then disappear. He finished the coffee in his cup, stubbed out the cigarette in the saucer, got up and went to the window. He drew back the curtain and looked out at the bleak morning with the sky dull and grey.

What Colette Didn't Know

No flies out this morning, he thought as he stood taking in the scene. The pigeons flew about from chimney-pot to chimney-pot on the roofs of the houses across the street. The crows cawed as they flew from the woods south of the city to the countryside in search of food. Hans knew that after crossing the city they would follow the course of the river Nidda to their destination. The tall lindens that line the middle of the avenue looked bear and ghostly stripped of their foliage. There were lights in some windows of the houses opposite, and Hans could almost see into the rooms. Not like in summer when the trees, green and fresh, you almost got the impression you were living in a park. Twill probably snow soon, he thought, and sure enough the first white flakes began to fall. The streetlamps were still on and the snowflakes danced around them like moths around a candle in a hot summer's night.

Two men in orange-coloured overalls were sweeping the pavement. One of them had an orange-coloured cap tightly tied around his head. The other man had some kind of cap with a knitted scarf pulled over it and muffled well round his face. Both were wearing gloves. They brushed the rubbish together into little piles and a third man came after them collecting it with a small brush and shovel. He threw the rubbish into a plastic bag which was hanging in a kind of small trolley with two wheels. The men worked efficiently trying to keep themselves warm and only seldom exchanged a word or two. Further up the street there was a small lorry parked at the crossing with its lights flashing. There was a time, when at this time of morning, apart from a quick glance out of the window, to see what the weather was like, Hans would have had no time for standing around looking out of the window. Instead, he'd be getting ready to go to work. But today he had time, and he was, to a certain extent glad, that the ice was finally broken, because, with winter approaching, he was finding it more and more difficult to fill in his day. Hans opened the window and let a loud sneeze. Shit!, he said, hope I'm not getting a cold. Then feeling a rumbling in his stomach, he quickly closed the window and made off for the bathroom. Some minutes later with the stink almost suffocating him he asked himself, Was that wine or turpentine I drank last night?

The radio was on, but Hans wasn't listening. for

What Colette Didn't Know

now, the whole extent of his mistake became clear to him. Why the bloody hell did I have to let it come to this? Why couldn't I have told Colette before now, before she found it out for herself? He poured the rest of the coffee into the cup and gulped it down standing. Then taking the cups and coffee-pot into the kitchen he said in a loud voice as if talking to the radio commentator, The game's up. After doing the wash-up he turned the radio off and went for a shower.

In the large mirror in the bedroom smelling of aftershave Hans saw himself naked. Looking at himself he thought, Maybe I ought to try and get work as a model. Then balancing on one leg he raised his hands above his head posing like one of Degar's ballet dancers. He dropped his leg - almost losing his balance - and turning sideways away from the mirror he said out loud, No, no, ladies, if you wish, by all means you may sketch my back. My bottom too, of course, I'm sure you'll relish it. But no private parts, please. Pulling on his boxers and carefully tucking in his balls he continued, Well, if you think your sketch will look better with my balls dangling in it, then you can have a go at them as well, ha, ha, ha. After buttoning up his shirt his hand reached for a

Mike Crowley

tie. Whoops! he exclaimed, pulling back his hand, No tie today sir. And with Colette's words still ringing in his ears, he went back to the living-room where he moped about looking at books. Finally he took the folder with the manuscript of his novel and sat down on the sofa. Poor Colette, he sighed, I can understand her anger. Like myself, she too never thought that it would come to this.

Chapter 2

Hans was from a small town in the north of Hesse. His father had worked till he was sixty-five, and his mother... All the stories she used to read to himself and his brother when they were young. They were from Sudentenland and came to Germany after The Second World War. Before coming to Germany his father had worked in a bank, and it was there that his mother met her husband. The couple brought one child, a son with them to Germany. His father soon found work with the local bank. His mother stayed at home looking after little Horst. All three lived in a small room with cooking facilities and no bathroom; this and the lavatory were outside in the landing. In those days it was difficult to get any kind of accommodation, because, due to the war, many of the houses were either bombed or damaged, making them unfit for living in. And then there were so many people, like his parents, looking for a place to stay. Round about a year later, when Hans was born, the family moved into a three-room flat. They would have liked a bigger place, but three rooms were all they could get till some years later. His mother wanted to take a course of German studies, but had to break it off because of the war. With the new flat and a second-hand typewriter, she turned to writing children stories.

Hans and his brother Horst were as different from each other as chalk and cheese, so that if you didn't know they were related, you would never have taken them for brothers. Their parents too, of course, were very much aware of this, and Mr Konrad senior could not altogether rid himself of suspicions. On the other hand both parents took a more than casual interest in Darwinism, so they understood that such things can happen. "Some unfortunate far-off ancestor of ours, I suppose" his father would joke, and let it at that. Horst was a

What Colette Didn't Know

rather low-sized chubby fellow with the build of a boxer, though he couldn't even hurt a fly. And if you happened to meet him in the night you might well have mistaken his face for a harvest moon. Besides he wasn't so bright at school and all he looked forward to was to get a job and have a quiet life. Hans on the other hand was quite the opposite. He was thin and hardy, ambitious and witty. He spent most of his time reading, adventure books being his favourites. As he got older he wondered if all what he read was true or were they only stories like his mother used to write. Well, he would find it out for himself some day, for he told himself that he would leave his home and see what the world was like. There were times too when he even tried writing short stories. These were stories about his dreams when he would grow up. After his leaving cert Hans decided to go and study in Frankfurt.

Horst, following his father's footsteps, went into banking in Frankfurt. He had a small flat not very far from the university. Horst was delighted to hear that Hans was coming to Frankfurt, because, though Horst was a jolly kind of chap, he didn't seem to make friends easily, especially with the women. He told Hans he could stay with him till he found a flat. Whenever Horst went home on weekends, he talked a lot about Frankfurt, and he was sure Hans would find it a great place to study. Hans quickly found a room in a student hostel not far from the university.

During the summer break, Hans took on a job for four or five weeks after which he spent the money travelling in Italy and Greece. Greece was his favourite place because it was dirt cheap and the climate was fantastic. When he returned, he usually went to visit his parents, and of course to collect a little money.

After taking his degree in economics, Hans entered the company that fired him thirty years later. The department manager at the time, long since retired with a fat pension, soon recognized that Hans was a person that was going places, and was prepared to work hard for it. He was undoubtedly a career man. As time passed, both men got along well together. Gradually he began climbing the ladder of success, going from project manger to group manager, and in time to department manager. The company too had invested a lot in him. He was regularly sent to special seminars for management training, courses on rhetoric, even spending some time in Ireland

What Colette Didn't Know

learning English. In those days there was no talk about flexibility or lean management, not to mention globalisation.

The morning he came back after a two weeks honeymoon he found a rather suspicious looking letter among the papers on his desk. It was from the personal recruiting office addressed to Mr Hans Konrad, department manager, and marked private. He sat down and pushing the other papers aside, took the letter and slit open the envelope with his ivory letter-opener; a birthday present from the staff. Quickly glancing through the letter a chill ran down his spine and his newly acquired suntan turned the colour of ashes. After reading it again and making quite sure the letter was for him (he was the only person he knew with that name in the company), he sank into the leather upholstered chair, and for a short while became oblivion to everything around him. The letter you see, was his dismissal.

Coming to himself again and still holding the letter in his hand, Hans said to himself, What the hell is this all about, some kind of bloody joke? Thirty years in the company and now fired. Just like that! I wonder if anybody knows about it?

Mike Crowley

Hans looked at the date on the letter. It was from Friday. Today was Monday. What will the people say? Hans Konrad fired? Unbelievable! After taking a deep breath, he put the letter back into the envelope and locked it into his desk. He then got up and went to see if his boss was in the office.

Tapping courteously on the open door before preceding into the room, Hans said, Good morning, Gerd.

Neuheimer, who was pouring over some papers looked up. Rising to his feet and holding out his hand in welcome he said, Oh, hallo Hans! Good morning. So our holiday-maker is back, and motioning with his hand for Hans to take a seat said, how are you, Hans and how was the holiday? Good weather, I suppose.

Gerd Neuheimer had joined the company the same year as Hans had, so they grew up together there. Neuheimer though, through some lucky chance had got on better than Hans, for he was only five years in the company when he got the position of group supervisor. Five years later he advanced to department manager. Then some ten years later he became senior head of department. It was at that time that Hans took over Neuheimer's position as department manager.

What Colette Didn't Know

Hans let his 75 odd kilos fall into the chair and patted his hair with his hand, now not so dark as it used to be.

Cigarette, Hans?

No, thanks, he replied, taking a packet from his pocket, try these ones. Greek, and continued, if I had known what was awaiting me, I wouldn't have come back at all.

Oh, you're referring to the letter, I suppose. Well, my dear Hans, to tell you the truth, the first thing I myself heard about it was on Friday last. Schilling's secretary phoned and said,

"Mr Schilling wants to see you at eleven o'clock in his office."

"The news isn't good," Schilling began and handing me a paper, "read that," he said, "it's a copy of this letter here," pointing to the blue envelope on his desk.

What's happened at all,? I asked him, after glancing through the letter.

"I'm sorry," said Schilling, "but these are orders from above."

He then leaned over his desk as if letting me into a secret. "As you know Mr Neuheimer, the board met a week ago. It was decided that due to the newly implemented software for the work in your department we must cut staff. Besides there was a lot of discussion about lean management. And I can assure you that this letter here is only the beginning."

Mr Neuheimer looked Schilling in the eyes and said, Are you somehow hinting Mr Schilling that I too might soon have to take my hat?

"Oh, gosh, no. I shouldn't look at it like that, Mr Neuheimer, but changes there'll be and this is but the tip of the iceberg."

I kept the letter with me and put it on your desk just before leaving on Friday, so I don't imagine that anyone has seen it.

How very considerate of you, Gerd, Hans said. Then Gerd glanced at his watch.

Oh, he said, grabbing a bundle of papers from his desk, and getting to his feet, five to eight. And ushering Hans out of the office, he said, Excuse me Hans, but I've a meeting at eight. We'll have as usual our department meeting at nine.

Hans went back to his office, sat down at his desk and lit a cigarette.

In his position Hans was well aware of the fact that changes were in sight and that this was bound to mean that people would be put off. It wasn't the

What Colette Didn't Know

first time. But that he was on the list, he thought, maybe the episode of a few years back might very well have contributed to his dismissal. It happened that his long time secretary left the company shortly after getting married, so Hans had to find a new secretary. When the new secretary began work, Hans introduced her to the staff. Some days later it was rumoured that he took her out to dinner that same Friday evening, and afterwards wanted her to go to a hotel with him.

Monday morning neither the new secretary nor Hans showed up for work. At the usual nine o'clock meeting Neuheimer appeared to inform the staff that Hans would be in later. And by the way, Neuheimer added, Mrs Klein is no longer secretary. We'll meet again later today and give you more information. If there are any problems, refer to me. For the moment everything was a little chaotic, because at least among the staff nobody knew for sure what had happened.

During the following days the matter of his dismissal was discussed with the personal office, but neither Neuheimer nor Schilling could do anything to keep Hans in the company. As a long standing employee however, he was entitled to six months notice, but because they wanted him out

as quickly as possible, he had to go the end of that month. It was agreed to pay him his salary till the end of the year, besides he was given a lump sum as well.
That's all very well, Hans complained, but I'll soon be out of a job. What a damned lot. They can all go and kiss my arse. That evening Colette met him at the door.
How did your day go, dearie,? she asked, throwing her arms round his neck.
Hans, when he was free again to talk, replied, Not good at all, Colette, some great changes since I left for holidays. He closed the door and remained standing with Colette still hanging round his neck.

I'm fed up with the job, he said. Just back from holidays and nothing but the same old stress and trouble. Now that I'm just turned 55, I'd much prefer to quit and go and tell the bastards they can keep their bloody job. I'll quit, Colette, and that will finish it. But then like someone that didn't quite believe his own words, he said, Well, Colette, I'll think about it anyway, you know it might even be a good thing to do. That way I would have more time for my writing. Colette tightened her hold on his neck.

What Colette Didn't Know

Oh, yes Hansy, and then we could get a flat in New York and we might even be able to afford a smaller one in Paris. And you could write in one room and I'd type the manuscripts in another. Wouldn't that be great, Hansy?

It sure would, Colette, and then to himself, poor Colette, you don't know what's awaiting us. But shaking off the triste thought, he said, Anyway Colette, I can tell you that from tomorrow on, I'm going to start cutting down my hours in that job.

And that you got married, were they all surprised?

You should have seen their faces, Colette, cooling off a bit.

I can well imagine. Never expected something like that, she said, kissing Hans.

Did they ask about me? I mean your wife? Where she's from…?

Ah, stop it Colette, they wouldn't ask questions like that.

I'll have to give you a photo of myself for your desk, she said, looking into his eyes, that would tease them, don't you think?

I don't know why I should want to tease them, Colette, Hans said laughing, but I'll gladly accept your offer. Indeed, how awfully silly of me, that

Mike Crowley

I didn't think about it myself, dear. All too new, my dear, only your first day back after our marriage, Colette said, smiling. Dinner will be served right away. Then he went and set the alarm clock a hour later. So Hans decided there was to be no more overtime or any kind of extra work for him. And as he had quite a lot of extra hours, he decided to see the job as little as possible. This was fine with Colette because she could sleep on longer in the mornings.

Chapter 3

Colette got off the tram at the centre and disappeared into the U-Bahn. It was nice and warm down there and there was light everywhere, a sharp contrast to the drab morning outside. People too seemed suddenly to appear from nowhere. Some standing at the baker's stall getting rolls for their breakfast. Others came out of the newspaper shop with the morning paper under their arm or held it open to have a quick look at the headlines before folding it and putting it into their briefcase or shopping bag. Two security men were standing chatting in a corner and a dobermann lying on the

Mike Crowley

ground beside them. It had a muzzle on. Passing the coffee shop Colette saw people sitting at the tables hugging hot cups of coffee. She took the escalator down to the platform to get the commuter.

Actually I shouldn't be here at all, she thinks. Last night I told myself I wouldn't go in to work this morning. I'd just ring them and say I'm sick. And now here I am waiting for my commuter. Of course, I could still just turn on my heels this minute and go up to the coffee shop and sit around there till the shops open. Or later maybe go to the library, take a book and sit in a quiet corner. Nice and cosy in there too.

She looked up as the commuter rolled into the platform. She pushed her way in like the others trying to grab a seat where they could read the newspaper in peace. She managed to get a seat at the window, after a lanky young man pulled in his legs to let her pass. Thanks, she said, attempting a smile, planking herself onto the seat. The man grinned and continued reading as the commuter moved off, jogging along underneath the city. Most people's heads were hidden behind newspapers. The fellow sitting opposite her had a small notebook open on his knee. From time to

What Colette Didn't Know

time he wrote something into it, then lifted his head with his eyes closed. He's thinking. He opens his eyes again and goes on writing. When Colette looked at him with his eyes closed, she thinks, his brain is working rapidly.

If I hadn't been on that plane, would I still have met Hans? Probably not. But there again, who knows? Is our fate planned? The place we live in, places we visit, the people we meet, friends and foes? Did Hans have to be on that plane at that time? And the way he went about tracking me down. Cute devil! My hazel eyes had hypnotized him, and my auburn hair did the rest. And that he prefers cherries to grapefruit. I had to laugh thinking what cherries and grapefruit had to do with my looks. I didn't ask him. Thought he was just trying to impress me being a kind of poetic.

At the Main station many people got off and as many more got on, some pulling suitcases. Holiday-makers, and of course business people bound for the airport. The commuter moved off again, now gathering speed as it climbed out of the tunnel into the dark morning, and passing over the river Main Colette shivered looking down at the cold murky water.

Mike Crowley

With all the hustle and bustle going on around her, Colette forgot about Hans for awhile. But looking out at the eerie morning and the naked trees, Hans crossed her mind again, and with him the fierce row of the night before. Oh!, it's snowing, she thinks, trying to keep him at bay. It just wasn't fair of him. Why couldn't he have told me about it right from the start? He didn't want to upset me. Bullshit! What the hell does he take me for? We're married and living together and...Well, he doesn't know much about me and I know just as much about him. But god damn it to hell! She turned from the window and looked round the compartment as if half afraid that the people might be able to read her thoughts. Didn't wash my hair either this morning. Must look terrible. Too confused. Well, I'm not at work yet. Just then the shrill sound of the train whistle signalled that they are entering the airport tunnel. Getting restless, the passengers folded their newspapers and started for the doors. Same scurrying every morning, she thought, rising to her feet and joining the crowd.

Outside on the platform she had to push her way through the jungle of people and suitcases to get to the escalator, hoping that no one would step on

What Colette Didn't Know

her toes or bump their case against her legs. One flight up it was still very busy with people rushing round in all directions. But by the time she finally reached the main hall of terminal one things had cooled off a bit. She walked on past the long rows of check-in desks and shops to catch the commuter to terminal two. The check-in desk wasn't open yet, but already there was a small group of people lined up at the baggage security check, before preceding to the check-in.

Bon jour, Jasmin, Colette said, throwing her handbag onto the desk, and slipping out of her overcoat.

Hi, Colette, she said, looking up from the magazine she was reading, still snowing? Colette pinned her ID-card to her blouse in front of a small mirror. Snow,? she said.

Yeah, it was snowing when I was coming to work.

Oh!, that's right, but not very much.

She took her handbag and swinging it over her shoulder went to the Ladies. Sitting alone she thought, That's when it happened. Hans used to take a glass or two, but I never saw him drunk till then. Talking about quitting the job. Needed more time for writing. He never once showed me what

Mike Crowley

he was writing. And I like a fool falling for it all; trips to New York and all that.

Jasmin thought, there's something wrong with Colette this morning. Somehow she's not herself. Her hair not done, and her face…Well, you'd think, she was crying all night. When she returned, Jasmin made no remarks. Acting as if she didn't notice anything, she stood up, took her handbag from the back of the chair and checked her face in the mirror. Leaving the office for the check-in desk Colette wonders, if she shouldn't tell Jasmin.

Chapter 4

It was just only about seven or eight months before Hans was fired, that he was sent to Korea. The board had chosen him to set up and implement the company's new project at their offices in Seoul. All had agreed that Hans was the best man for the job. He was one of the team that had developed and successfully introduced the project in Frankfurt. On his return after a two weeks stay, Hans called a meeting of the bosses for that same afternoon to give them a report on his journey and a presentation of how he had succeeded with the project. At the end of the presentation and having answered the questions asked, Hans got a rousing round of applause. Some even came and shook his hand patting him on the back as if he had just informed them that he had won an Olympic gold medal.

That morning there was the usual weekly department meeting. Mr Neuheimer, who was managing the department while Hans was away, brought him up to date on matters regarding general developments. More specific matters would be dealt with in Neuheimer's office at the eleven o'clock meeting. After the meeting which barely lasted half an hour, Hans went back to his office and was glad that neither Neuheimer nor any of the staff had delayed him with queries. Looking through the pile of papers on his desk, Hans put those that weren't urgent into the tray marked CAN WAIT. Papers he considered not important went straight into the wastepaper basket, and the rest he arranged according to priority. After lighting a cigarette, he poured himself a coffee. Then he set about preparing the presentation for that afternoon.

Hans had often told himself, if he gets involved in all sorts of possible projects in the company,

What Colette Didn't Know

the chances are that he'd be kept on till retirement. Yes, even perhaps a better chance of further promotion. Just show them you're important. That's the whole secret.

It was arranged that Hans fly out from Paris, where he had spent most of the week consulting with colleagues at their Paris office, instead of returning to Frankfurt and flying to Korea from there. He had worked long hours putting the final touches to his new project, so during that flight he decided to take advantage of the situation, give himself a little break from all that paperwork, and spend some of the flight time working on his novel, because he had to admit that with all that work he had neglected his writing, and now he saw an opportunity to catch up with the story. Besides, this would be a kind of mental recreation taking his mind away from facts and figures into the world of fiction. So after lunch was served, he set to work with pen and paper. He had often heard that many writers work directly typing into a PC. But he didn't approve of this. At least not for himself anyway. He needed the feel of paper and pen to guide him through the world of fiction. Staring into a monitor was somehow too modern

Mike Crowley

to stimulate fiction.

He worked away steadily becoming oblivion to what was happening around him. Then somewhere along the line feeling a little tired, he stopped writing, and read through what he had written. As he did so, he noticed the plane was losing altitude. He checked his watch, wondering how long more it was till landing. Half an hour to go, he thought, stretching out his legs and straightening himself in his seat. It was then he looked up, and glancing about him found himself staring into the eyes of a stewardess standing in the aisle. Something stirred somewhere deep inside Hans, and he had a feeling that the woman with the hazel eyes had the same feeling. Christ! Darwinian chaos, he thought, did I have to travel to the other side of the globe for this chemistry jerk? The stewardess quickly recovered and got on with her work. But Hans, with a dry mouth and another thirty minutes to go, decided he must have a drink. He pressed the button.

Yes sir, What can I do for you?

Hans swallowed and held onto the arms of his seat, while the hazel eyes stood staring into his.

Can I have a whiskey soda, please?

Certainly, sir. And she was gone, Hans follow-

What Colette Didn't Know

ing every swagger of her bottom. Seconds later placing the drink on the table she said: There you are, sir, and turned away quickly, as if suddenly confronted with an overpowering force. Thanks, he said, but she was gone, his eyes followed her again. He gulped down the whiskey, poured the soda into the glass and sent it down after it. Shit! missed my chance. He actually thought he could have a word with her, but everything went too fast.

Meanwhile the cabin crew was busy getting ready for landing. They walked up and down the aisles checking to see if the safety belts were fastened and the seats were in a upright position. Hans considered pressing the service bell again and calling another drink to see if she would come again. He could certainly do with another drink, he thought, but on second thoughts decided against it. Maybe I should write the hotel phone number on my visiting card, press the service button and give it to her. Or I could hand it to her leaving the plane. On the other hand, he thought, what would I be doing with a stewardess? They're scooting around the world every day meeting rich men. And I? What have I to offer one like that? Well, I suppose, doing no harm by giving her my card anyhow.

There was a slight bump as the plane touched down on the tarmac and taxied to the arrivals building. "Ladies and Gentlemen, welcome to Seoul. Please remain seated with your seat belts fastened till the aircraft has reached its final position and the signs have been switched off." Hans looked out of the window as the voice continued from the loudspeaker. Finally the plane came to a halt and with it the click, click, click of seatbelts being opened, the passengers got to their feet, taking their hand baggage from the overhead bins. Hans followed, mechanically reaching for the small leather bag containing a laptop and two or three notebooks, still wondering how to contact the girl. He put the folder with the manuscript into the bag. Then with the bag and his overcoat over his arm he left the plane, the card with the phone number of the hotel for the stewardess still in his hand. Walking along the gangway to the arrivals hall, Hans wasn't quite sure if he had even said bye to the crew members. Nothing worked out as he had planned it. He followed on through passport control, on to pick up his luggage and out to the taxi stand, from where he was taken to his hotel.

What Colette Didn't Know

In his hotel room Hans took a quick shower. Then after pulling on a loose cotton shirt and trousers, he stored his laptop and manuscript in the safe, and took the lift to the bar in the spacious lobby. There he ordered whiskey and soda, lit a cigarette and was just settling back to enjoy his drink when he saw a group of airliners enter the hotel, each pulling a suitcase on wheels and without looking right or left they walked up to the reception. All routine for them, he thought, keeping his eyes on them. Blast it!, if that's not the crew I just came with. That was her without doubt. He drank the whiskey, jumped up from the table leaving the soda untouched and started off towards the lift where the crew stood waiting.

When the lift came, Hans let them in first, then followed behaving as if taking no notice of them. One of them pressed the floor number, and off they went. This was easy, he thought, there're all going to the same floor. When the lift stopped, Hans stepped out, again pretending no interest. But in fact, it was quite the contrary for, as they set off looking for their rooms, Hans kept a sharp eye on the stewardess with the hazel eyes, following her at a convenient distance. When she found her room, she opened the door and went in without looking round. Got you now, he chuckled, sneaking up to look at the room number, which he scrawled on his cigarette-box, quickly skipping off back to the lift and down to the lobby bar, where he ordered another drink.

His empty glass and bottle of soda water were no longer on the table. Relaxing in a low chair Hans lit a cigarette, blew the smoke high into the air, poured some of the soda into the whiskey and took a sip. Well done, Hans, he praised himself, but now I'll have to act quickly, because, for all I know, she could be gone again by tomorrow. He stood up, walked to a small table beside the reception, took a sheet of hotel writing-paper and an envelope and returned to his drink. Hmmm…? let's see now, he thought, taking a pen from his shirt pocket, I'll have to write this in English, for I don't suppose she knows German. That does it. He folded the letter, put it into the envelope, sealed it, wrote the room number on it and handed it in at the reception. Then he went to his room.

Hallo stewardess,

I was on the flight from Paris with you. I

What Colette Didn't Know

>love your hazel eyes. I was sitting at the window next to that fellow, probably Korean, that drank so much beer. If you happen to be in Frankfurt anytime, you might give me a buzz. I'd love to see you again sometime. Kindest regards, Hans

Actually Hans had never really intended getting married. His love of adventure which as a boy he had experienced from reading remained with him as a grown up. He valued his freedom, as he said, and women only hamper a man's life. He didn't want to have a woman waiting for him when he came home in the evenings. He wanted to be able to come and go as he willed, free from all kinds of fetters. But just like Samson had his weak points, so too had Hans Konrad.

Chapter 5

Some two or three weeks later when Colette woke in her flat in Paris, the light coming through the curtains told her it must be day. She stretched out in the bed to her full length of one hundred and sixty-eight centimetres, and half loud, half to herself said, That was a sleep! Then she turned to look at the clock, that told her it was coming up to midday. She got up, went for a pee, and back into bed. She tucked the blankets around her and put her hands under her neck. Four days off, she sighed, just great, smiling up at the light blue ceiling. The walls were a soft shade of yellow.

Mike Crowley

From the bed she could see herself in the mirror of the wardrobe. No alarm clock, no planes, no passengers, no hotel beds.

She had treated herself to a long sleep because she was simply jaded. So, she thought, what am I going to do with my day, or at least with what's left of it? Well now, let's see...I could, for example, stay in bed all day. No, that wouldn't be fun. Maybe I should call up some friends? Here she baulked. Friends? That's the biggest problem with us airliners. Oh, sure, we meet the world of people, but it's hard to hold on to friends in our job. Either we're working when our friends are off or it's vice versa. And as for boyfriends? No trouble getting them, but they soon lose interest, saying we're never around when they want us. And besides they're very jealous, always thinking that when we're away we have someone else screwing us.

Colette took her hands from under her head and tucked them in under the blankets for her arms were getting cold. Friends, she repeated, friends! Suddenly she threw back the blankets and jumped out of bed. She went around and turned the heating up, and tying her dressing-gown around her, she went to the window. The sky over Paris

What Colette Didn't Know

looked mucky. Below on the street people walked about, in and out of the shops, or stood looking at the shop windows.

It was a small flat with two rooms, kitchen and bathroom. The two rooms were at one-time one large room now divided by a wall, which was not part of the original building. The rooms were connected by an arch-shape opening, which Colette didn't even bother to separate by a curtain. The kitchen was small too. It contained a small gas cooker, a fridge, an aluminium sink and a cup board on the wall. From the window you looked into the kitchens of the neighbouring flats. In the bathroom there was a shower and the washing machine she had brought with her. When Colette moved in she bought a little folding table with a Formica top for preparing food. She kept vegetables and tins in a trolley. Fruit she had in a shallow wooden bowl on the table in the living-room.

Colette came from Colmar. A sleepy town in Alsace with frame-work houses, cobble-stone streets, quaint little shops and renowned for its wines, gastronomy and gourmet restaurants. She grew up in a picturesque scenery, scampering about Petite Venise with its walks along the banks of the river Lauch. Picnics in the summer in the nearby village of Wintzenheim, and later when she got a bike, cycling out there with her friends to scout about the woods and vineyards.

Her first visit to Paris was with the school. God, was that exciting! We went there by train. It all looked so huge. High buildings everywhere you looked and long wide streets. Colette had never seen anything like it before. Not even in Strassbourg, where she went to secondary school. That time they went to see some of the most important sites. There was Louvre with its gardens and monuments and a long queue of people waiting to go in. But lucky for us, we were ushered in through a side-door. Mona Lisa was the big attraction, but it was hard to get to see it with so many people and it was hidden behind safety glass. Then on to Arc de Triomphe, the Eiffel Tower, Notre Dame, Sacré Coeur, the Panthéon, the Bastille and a short boot trip on the Seine. More wasn't in it in our three days stay.

Now, here she was in Paris thinking about spring, when it was still only December, as she turned

What Colette Didn't Know

away from the window. She took a bundle of underwear from a basket in the bedroom and marched off with it into the bathroom. She put the clothes into the washing machine, threw in some powder, turned on the water and then turned on the machine. After preparing a big mug of milk coffee, she carried it in both hands into the living-room and put it on a small table beside the sofa, then she planked herself onto the sofa. She bent over and sipped the hot drink again holding the mug in both hands. She put the mug back on the table, reached for her handbag lying beside her, threw one leg over the other and leaned back. She rooted in her handbag for her notebook, found it, and there next to it was a letter. Wondering, she took it and saw a hotel room number on the envelope.

When she was given it at the hotel reception in Seoul, she had glanced quickly at it, and as it wasn't important, she had just put it into her handbag and forgotten about it. She took out the letter and read: Hans Konrad, an address in Frankfurt and a telephone number. Hmmm, another one of these fellows, she laughed, it happens all the time in our job. Some give you their card with "please get in touch". Others would love to invite you out to dinner. Then you sometimes find a letter at the hotel reception, like this one, telling you they'd like a date with you. All imagining we're easy to get, just waiting to be screwed. That things happen, I'll grant you, but we are by no means a bunch of flying whores!

Colette let the letter fall onto the sofa as she bent over to finish her coffee, now not so hot anymore. A weak ray of sunshine entered through the window and spread all over the room. "I'm sure you still remember the collision of our eyes." In the quietness, Colette hears the drone of the washing machine as she recalls the passenger with the slim, straight nose and smiling eyes. Oh yes, I remember all right. Almost flattened me. Good-looking fellow to be sure...not so very young though...late forties...maybe. I wonder what my parents would say to that? About half his age. She laughed out loud at the idea, but she could see the eyes smiling at her. He spent a lot of the flight writing, she recalls. Wouldn't be a writer by any chance, would he? Oh, god, let's hope not one of those fellows. All of them a bit crazy. Talking about their characters as if they were real people. All stony mad! No, none of that sort, I hope. Besides, I doubt if they'd be travelling business-

What Colette Didn't Know

class. No, most probably a businessman. Writing reports or something like it. Good position too, I suppose, no danger of losing his work. Lucky fellow with all that unemployment. Come to think of it, even our job isn't safe today. The sun was gone again, so Colette bent over and switched on the little lamp beside the sofa. That's better, she said to herself, and continued reading. "What a coincidence for the two of us to be in the same hotel." Yes, indeed, quite a coincidence. But how the devil did he get my room number? And strange that he didn't try to contact me then. Too busy, maybe.

After her leaving cert Colette went to Ireland to work as au pair. She lived with a family outside of Dublin and she had to travel into Dublin city three times a week to attend English classes. A great change for Colette. No vineyards anywhere but the sea ever present. At first she found it difficult to understand the people. Their English did not sound like the English her teacher had spoken at school. But gradually her ears adapted, and she soon could understand the people quite well. Colette wanted to improve her English because she intended to apply for work at Air France. When she told her parents about it, they agreed

Mike Crowley

that it was a very wise idea. Unemployment was becoming more and more a reality and a job with the air lines was not only interesting but secure as well. "Sure it's taking on people they are instead of sacking them," her mother said. And though her parents were aware of the fact that Colette, their only child, would probably have to move to Paris for training, they were glad she had made such a good choice. While still in Ireland Colette wrote to Air France requesting information.

Colette threw off her dressing-gown and flung it onto the bed. Under the shower she wondered if she would get through standby without any hitches. She was tired and badly needed the few days off. She dried herself and tied a dry towel around her hair. Meanwhile the washing machine was finished. She turned off the water, took the clothes and hung them on the clothes-horse. After drying her hair and doing her make-up, she got dressed and went out, leaving the letter behind on the table.

Chapter 6

Hans put his briefcase down on the doorstep. He pulled a bunch of keys out of his overcoat pocket and opened the letterbox. A letter from Deutsche Telekom, a bill, he muttered, flyers from some travel agents and a letter. He turned it over to see who it was from. Colette Gilbert, Paris. Hans looked at it and knitted his forehead. No, he thought, shaking his head, don't know anyone with that name. He let the flyers in the box, took the letters and his briefcase, and went up to his flat.

On his way to the office that morning, Hans

thought about the Paris office. He would have to go there once more before Christmas, he knew. How time flies, he mused, the year is almost finished, and spring still a long way off. Spring was his favourite season with the birds singing and the bright mornings. There was something exhilarating about it that no other season could offer.

That morning he sat at his desk staring at a report which he held in both hands. He wasn't reading it, for his thoughts had turned to the manuscript he was writing. Yes, he had managed to finish that chapter the previous evening. And what a stubborn chapter it was. Hans paused, and chuckled. A stubborn chapter, he repeated, I damn well nearly wanted to throw in the lot. Grab the sheets, run down the stairs and dump the lot into the waste-paper bin. Yes, that's just what he would have liked to do with it. The phone rang. Hans let fall the report onto the desk, cleared his throat and reached out his hand to take the receiver.

Konrad, good morning!

Baum, morning boss!

Hallo, Mrs Baum, what can I do for you?

Boss, I'm just reading here that you'll be thirty

What Colette Didn't Know

years with the company in October. My goodness, how time passes! I was ...

I'm sure we'll have time enough to talk about that later, I'm busy now looking through that report.

Okay, Boss, have a nice day.

Hans put back the receiver. Thirty years with the company and I don't regret a day of it. So, that leaves me only ten years to go till retirement. He smiled, content with himself as he rubbed his chin with his hand. Perfect planning, Hans, he said to himself.

He turned on the light in the hall and dropped his briefcase behind the door. He went into the living-room, switched on the light and put the letter, the keys and his reading glasses on the table. Then he went round and turned up the heating. He hung his overcoat on the coat-stand, removed his shoes and pulled on his slippers. He hung his suit jacket over a chair in the bedroom and returned to the living-room. He sat on the sofa, lit a cigarette, put on his glasses. He then picked up the letter and read the name out loud, Colette Gilbert. Never heard of her. Maybe someone in our offices in Paris, he said to himself, opening the envelope, but why write to me? It's in German, he said to himself, quickly scanning the three lines of writing. Suddenly he burst out laughing and threw the letter into the air. Well, well, he said, repeating out loud what he read, "I'm the hotel room number in Seoul." Colette Gilbert, the hotel room number. Well, isn't that good! Hans recovered the letter from the floor, And she knows German as well. Colmar, so that's where she's from. Some fine restaurants down that way. Hans turned and looked towards the window where he saw it was pouring rain. Man, was that some night when Neuheimer took us to his birthday party in Colmar. His fiftieth birthday it was. My god, that was some feasting. And the mirabelle! I'll never forget it. He looked again at the window and, the rain, he thought, had eased off. Colette Gilbert, he repeated to himself, my little hazel eyes stewardess. Well, here goes Hans, another flirt, and a French one this time. Hans sank into the sofa. Whee, he made, all that excitement has given me an appetite, and I know exactly where to go. The Italian place round the corner. Pasta and red wine.

He put his glasses on the table, went and changed into a corduroy trousers and pullover, got into a pair of casual shoes and a leather jacket that

What Colette Didn't Know

had seen better days, collected his purse, keys and glasses and turned off the light.

The streets were still wet after the rain and the west wind pushed broken clouds across the evening sky. I don't understand why they closed that place, he thought, walking past the pub at the corner, now looking like a ghost house. It was such a good place and they seemed to be doing a good business. At the traffic lights he waited for the lights to change to green. There was a non-stop flow of cars out of the city. Commuters going home from work. When red brought the traffic to a halt, he crossed.

Hans was a regular at the restaurant. This didn't mean that he went there a few times a week. No!, but he went there often enough to be regarded as a regular. The waiters knew him and they also knew he had a very good job. Tonight, dressed as he was in casual wear, he looked as ordinary as the guests sitting at the other tables. But when he went there with business friends, all wearing well-trimmed suits and fashionable ties, the waiters recognized he was an important man.

Hans usually had his breakfast at home before going to work and at lunch he ate in the canteen. After work, if he didn't go out with colleagues or visiting colleagues from their offices abroad, he either prepared something at home or went out like tonight. Looking through the menu, he exchanged a few words with the waiter. He handed back the menu and said, But bring me a Chianti first. Hans looked round at the other tables, but didn't recognize anybody. Anyway, they didn't look like business people, too early for them yet, he thought. The waiter brought the wine, a mixed salad and sliced baguette.

Boun appetito!, he said.

Hans took a sip of the wine and began tucking in. The three waiters were all the time on the go. In and out of the kitchen carrying plates of pasta, salads, baguette and glasses of white and red wines. A couple sitting at a table on their own had ordered a bottle of red wine, but the table was too far away for Hans to see what wine they were drinking.

Careful, now, said the waiter placing a dish of piping hot cannelloni on the table.

Thanks, Luigi, he said, pulling back from the table. Again the waiter wished him buon appetito.

What's Colette doing now,? I wonder. Is she at home in her flat watching TV or reading a book, or maybe expecting that I might ring her? He took

What Colette Didn't Know

the glass and let the wine trickle slowly down his throat. I'll phone her tonight, he decided. I'll see if she's there and tell her I'll be in Paris the middle of next week. If Colette isn't working, we might be able to meet. He dipped the bread in the remaining sauce, and when he had finished eating, he wiped his lips with the paper serviette. And now for a smoke, he suggested, and his hand wandered into the pocket of his jacket hanging on the back of the chair. He leaned back inhaling the first pull and noticed he was the only one smoking.

Tutto bene,? the waiter asked collecting the empty plates.

Fine, Hans replied, it was very nice. Could you bring me another wine and the bill, please.

Okay, sir.

When he returned, Hans paid and tipped the waiter.

Grazie, signore, he said, and gave him his change.

When Hans finished his wine and a second cigarette, he said Good night, and left.

The west wind was still chasing the broken clouds from behind which the cold light of the moon appeared from time to time.

Chapter 7

The first time they met in Paris, Hans felt like a schoolboy going out on his first date. It was the second day of a business trip to Paris; incidentally the last meeting of the year. The previous evening the manager of their Paris offices invited Hans to dinner along with some two or three colleagues. Hans was their guest while in Paris, and he knew the next evening would be the same procedure. But Hans had different plans for that evening and so he had to tell the manager that, unfortunately he would not be able to go out with them that evening. Surprised, the manager looked up at him, for he knew that Hans enjoyed the evenings out with himself and some colleagues, and laughing said, Is there a pretty Parisian in the game?

No. no, Hans said, lying, and hoping he wasn't blushing, because he could feel his cheeks getting hot, it's just that I want to go to an exhibition, as it's my last visit to Paris this year.

Oh, so that's why, said the manager, sizing up Hans, and added, by the way, Hans, any sound of wedding bells in the offing?

Not that I know of, Hans answered, and thought about Colette.

Hans sat at the table with a glass of red wine. It was a small homely restaurant not far from where Colette lived. A young woman with black long hair stood behind the bar. Her lips were hidden behind a heavy coat of lipstick. She was talking with a man sitting on a high stool. He had a small glass in front of him on the bar, and Hans assumed it must be an aperitif. A waiter stood at a table beside the bar. He was folding paper serviettes. From time to time he took part in the conversation between the woman and the man at the bar. Usually this happened when one of them passed some remark that caused a laugh. He would stop

What Colette Didn't Know

folding the serviettes and make some comment at which they would all laugh again. Pity I don't know French, Hans thought, I'd love to know what their conversation is about.
After hanging his overcoat on the coat stand marked GARDE–ROBE, Hans chose a table at a large window with a narrow curtain on a brass pole. The curtain, though not of a thick material, was there to prevent the passers-by from looking into your plate while at the same time permitting those inside a view of what was happening outside on the street. The last time he had sat like this in a restaurant waiting for a woman was about five or six years ago. She left the company for a job in Hamburg. He got a postcard from her some weeks after going to Hamburg telling him she was settling in to her new life. After that he never heard from her again. That time there was all that talk about lean management. What's my date going to be like this evening, he thought, glancing at his watch.

From where he sat he had a good view of the door. This was important because, come to think of it, Hans had only seen Colette on the plane and later in the hotel and then only in her uniform. Would he recognize her without the uniform,? he wondered, looking out at the cold damp evening and the bright lights of the Christmas decorations. Just as he was about to light a cigarette, his attention was drawn towards the door and a young woman. Nervously Hans eyed her, looking her up and down. She wore no headgear and Hans at once recognized her auburn hair. It's Colette, he said to himself. The woman, while she stood unbuttoning her coat, glanced round at the tables as if she were looking for someone. Once again the waiter stopped folding the serviettes and went to help her out of the coat and hung it on the coat stand. She wore jeans, a black polo-neck jersey and black low-heeled shoes. Her shoulder bag was black too. Hans felt his heart beat faster as he watched her chatting with the waiter, holding her gloves in both hands.

A local, he thought, taking the cigarette from his lips and placing it in the ashtray before getting up and going over to the woman. Hallo, Colette, he said, hoping he was right and, at the same moment startled at his own courage. The young woman looked at him and stretched out her hand. Colette Gilbert, she said, shaking his hand. Despite the cool weather, her hand was warm in his. She then said something to the waiter, of which Hans only

What Colette Didn't Know

understood monsieur Konrad, and the waiter held out his hand. They shook hands and Hans ushered Colette to the table.

So you found the place, Colette started, taking a seat opposite Hans.

Oh, it was no trouble at all, Colette, I took the metro. I don't have to tell you about the traffic in Paris at this time of evening.

Colette put her gloves into her bag and hung it on the back of the chair.

True, she said, smiling at Hans.

They were the same eyes that made his cock erect while on the plane and here he was now gazing into them again.

Mind if I smoke, Colette,? he asked, settling himself into his chair. He picked up the cigarette from the ashtray, flicked the ash off and continued smoking.

No, she said, as long as you don't keep blowing the smoke into my face.

What would you like to drink,? he asked looking away from Colette and beckoning to the waiter, who was more or less waiting to be called.

What are you drinking, Hans?

It's a vin de pays, Colette, dry.

I'll have the same, she said, looking up at the

Mike Crowley

waiter.
 And the menu too, please, Hans added.
Colette didn't look at the menu. Instead she pulled up the sleeves of her jersey a little, rested her elbows on the table, and asked Hans how he got to find out the number of her room at the hotel in Seoul.

She sported a Swatch on her left wrist and a silver bracelet on her right arm. Hans noticed she had no rings on her fingers. He smiled at her like someone waiting for that question. He drew on his cigarette, then stubbed it out on the ashtray, put his elbows on the table and looking into her eyes said, Well, it was very easy. All I had to do was to follow you to your room. Colette laughed and thought, cute little devil.

Do you come to Paris often,? she asked raising her glass. Hans let the question hang in the air and took his glass too.

To your health! Colette.
The red dry table wine roused the saliva in Colette's mouth tickling her palate as she let it flow slowly down her throat. Hans smacked his lips and put the glass down on the table.

A few times a year, he said, my company has an office here.

What Colette Didn't Know

understood monsieur Konrad, and the waiter held out his hand. They shook hands and Hans ushered Colette to the table.

So you found the place, Colette started, taking a seat opposite Hans.

Oh, it was no trouble at all, Colette, I took the metro. I don't have to tell you about the traffic in Paris at this time of evening.

Colette put her gloves into her bag and hung it on the back of the chair.

True, she said, smiling at Hans.

They were the same eyes that made his cock erect while on the plane and here he was now gazing into them again.

Mind if I smoke, Colette,? he asked, settling himself into his chair. He picked up the cigarette from the ashtray, flicked the ash off and continued smoking.

No, she said, as long as you don't keep blowing the smoke into my face.

What would you like to drink,? he asked looking away from Colette and beckoning to the waiter, who was more or less waiting to be called.

What are you drinking, Hans?

It's a vin de pays, Colette, dry.

I'll have the same, she said, looking up at the

waiter.

And the menu too, please, Hans added.

Colette didn't look at the menu. Instead she pulled up the sleeves of her jersey a little, rested her elbows on the table, and asked Hans how he got to find out the number of her room at the hotel in Seoul.

She sported a Swatch on her left wrist and a silver bracelet on her right arm. Hans noticed she had no rings on her fingers. He smiled at her like someone waiting for that question. He drew on his cigarette, then stubbed it out on the ashtray, put his elbows on the table and looking into her eyes said, Well, it was very easy. All I had to do was to follow you to your room. Colette laughed and thought, cute little devil.

Do you come to Paris often,? she asked raising her glass. Hans let the question hang in the air and took his glass too.

To your health! Colette.

The red dry table wine roused the saliva in Colette's mouth tickling her palate as she let it flow slowly down her throat. Hans smacked his lips and put the glass down on the table.

A few times a year, he said, my company has an office here.

What Colette Didn't Know

Oh, so you know Paris then, she said.

I don't have much time for sightseeing, he continued, it's all work and no play.

I see, she said, and Hans thought he noticed a touch of sympathy in her voice.

But of course, Colette, I was here as a tourist, a long time ago though. However my short business trips help me to keep in touch.

I love Paris, Colette sighed, for me it's the most beautiful city in the world.

Hans listened to her picking away at his coq aux vin. Colette, he thought didn't seem hungry, for now she started off into a kind of monologue, telling Hans how she first came to Paris with the school. That she always wanted to become an airliner so she could see the world. Yes, and she went to Dublin to learn English. She liked it there and for a time thought about getting work there. She stopped talking, nibbled a little at her food, then took her glass and drank a toast to Hans. Seeing his chance, Hans drank quickly and said, So, you were in Dublin? I was there too many years ago.

You too? She exclaimed, looking into his eyes, so it seems, Hans, we have certain things in common, don't you think?

Mike Crowley

Meanwhile the other tables were occupied too. They all spoke French and from time to time someone would glance over at Colette and Hans speaking German. After enquiring of Hans where he had lived in Dublin and telling him all about her stay there, Colette wanted to know what he was doing in Seoul. Hans explained that he was department manager in the company, and that he was sent there to implement a new computer system.

Oh!, said Colette laughing, and on the plane I took you for a writer.

A writer? Hans asked, confused, what the devil made you think that?

Colette, still laughing said, Well, you spent so much time writing during the flight that you didn't even seem to notice me.

Oh, Colette, I'm really sorry about that. All my fault, but you'll forgive me, I hope. But still, I find it rather interesting that you should take me for a writer. My mother used to write children stories, and sometimes I think I'm taking after her.

He did not mention anything about the book he was working on.

Okay, she said, and by the way, when is our next date going to be?

What Colette Didn't Know

Hans, somewhat taken aback thought, this girl it seems, really means business.

A matter we'll have to think about, he said. The fact is that tomorrow is my last business trip to Paris for this year.

Oh!, is that so,? said Colette.

Well, no need to worry, Hans broke in, Frankfurt isn't all that far away from here.

I'll have to check out my flight schedule, she said, but I haven't it with me.

No problem, he said, I'll give you a ring tomorrow or after.

Good idea, she agreed, then stood up and taking her handbag said, I'm off to the Ladies.

Hans called the waiter and paid the bill. When she returned, Hans was putting the receipt into his purse. Getting up, he excused himself saying, I'm off to see a man about a dog.

Back again at the table he took a little silver box from his pocket, opened it and gave Colette his visiting card. Colette looked at it and read Hans Konrad and the name of the company. She made no comment, but took her bag and put the card into a little side pocket. That done, they drank off their wine.

I enjoyed our evening Colette, he said, and I

Mike Crowley

hope we'll have many more of them.
 I too, Hans, she said.
Outside Hans looked after her as she hurried home. And I'll have to sleep alone tonight, he thought, getting into a taxi.

Chapter 8

The game that began on that famous flight to Seoul turned into a wild love affair in the weeks that followed their first rendezvous in Paris. Hans went about as if floating on air, carried away with having found the woman he had been searching for. He laughed at the thought, because he was not sure, that it ever occurred to him he had been looking for such a woman to marry. This French girl was a sensation no doubt, and Hans fell head over heels in love with her, remembering, that it was himself got the whole thing rolling in the first place with the hotel room number. With a woman like Colette, he thought, I could soar happily through the years till my retirement. However, in the midst of all his excitement, Hans could see problems approaching, lots of problems.

It was great, he thought, that though they were from different countries, they could converse freely in the same language. The trouble was however, they were also living in different countries, which meant, of course, that they could not see each other as often as they would like to. Besides, Hans wondered as to how long an affair like this could go on under such circumstances. Would it all turn out to be a passing fancy? No, Hans told himself, I'll never allow it come to that. Whenever Colette was in Paris, Hans phoned her every day, and when she was away on flights, the SMS helped them to keep in touch.

But what if they decided to marry,? Hans asked himself, was Colette prepared to move to Frankfurt? Hans knew that it was very unlikely that he would go and live in Paris. After all he had a very secure job, a good position with that, and he did not know French. Hans laughed at it all and said, problems are there to be solved. Meanwhile Hans used every opportunity to go to Paris, and when he wasn't there on business, he travelled there by train on weekends. There were of course weekends when Colette had to work, because she was still on the Paris to Seoul flights.

When Hans proposed marriage just two months after they had met, Colette was slightly bent over, her arms resting on the table. She straightened herself, shifted her bottom on the chair and ran her fingers through her hair allowing herself time to digest what Hans had just said. Apparently taken aback by this sudden suggestion, Colette could only say, she would need some time to consider the matter. They were sitting in a café in the Gare d'Est station waiting for the train to take Hans back to Frankfurt. Hans was leaning against the chair-back smoking. Colette leaned over, took his hands and held them in her own. I'll think about it, she said, caressing his hands. Hans smiled at her and nodded. He released one of his hands, took the cigarette from his mouth, drank the rest of the coffee and stuck the cigarette back between his lips. Secretly Colette was thrilled with what Hans had said. This was the reassurance she loved to hear, that Hans was really in love with her, and was now suggesting marriage. While admitting she was madly in love with Hans, marrying him would bring some great changes into her life. For Hans it was crystal clear that Colette quit Paris and move to Frankfurt. A big problem for Colette though. Paris was her home and she loved it, and now for a new love she would have to sacrifice her other love, Paris. A tough decision, she thought, give up her work at Air France, and would she find work in Frankfurt? Hans had told her she didn't have to work. With his salary and secure job they could live quite comfortably. But Colette wondered how she was going to pass the days without work, and then what will it be like living in Frankfurt,? living with Hans? Colette had never before lived with a man for any length of time. Questions, questions as one day followed the next and Colette knew she had no other choice. A new life in a new country with a new man.

Chapter 9

The night before Colette came to live in Frankfurt, Hans could hardly close an eye. He kept on twisting and turning, switching the light on and off every half-an-hour to see what time it was. Finally, towards morning, when he began to dose off, the alarm clock rang. Hans turned it off, rolled over on his back, and lay there with his hands under his head. This was the day he was waiting for. His trips to Paris were worth it all, he thought, and tonight they would make love for the first time in his bed. And, with Colette here, he mused, I'll have more time on my hands and, who knows, with a little bit of luck, I might even get that director position. Goodbye to the weekend trips to Paris, which he had enjoyed to the full. It was of course a bad time of year for travelling but, with Amor firing him on, Hans had always undertaken the journey with the enthusiasm of a young lover.

In a sense, he had been able to kill two birds with the one stone. The trip offered him a pleasant time in Colette's small flat, and during the journey he could get through the office work he used to take home with him on weekends. Indeed, Hans was very glad of having something constructive to pass the time because, the journey all across France was not very picturesque in winter and early spring when the whole countryside was covered deep in snow and nothing much to see except the dull grey houses of the small towns and villages along the route, or the dark shape of a crow hacking away at the frozen ground trying to dig up something to eat. Hans pulled his hands from under his head and began to laugh, thinking about how, in the train, he used to turn his head away from the window and taking a drink from a Flachmann, his hip-flask, would say to his fellow-travellers, My elixir for cold scenery. After that he'd get down to his office work with his laptop

What Colette Didn't Know

resting on his knees.

It was during those weekend dates, short though they were, arriving late Friday night and away again on Sunday, that Colette and Hans got to know each other better. The anticipated pleasure of caressing Colette's soft, but firm breasts and being smothered with her juicy kisses pricked his cock, injecting it with a kind of frenzied hysteria. It was in this state of rhapsody that Hans, weather be damned, boarded the train for Paris. He kept the whole business a top secret, never once leaking out a word about it neither in the company nor to any of his friends at his local. Moreover, he caused no reason for any suspicion, as the trips weren't on a regular basis, so, if Hans didn't show up an odd Saturday evening, he wasn't the only one to do so, and his local remained closed on Sundays.

Hans turned to look at the clock. He stretched himself, and with a sudden sweep of his hand he threw back the bedclothes, and jumped out of bed.

Over in Paris Colette was up early that morning preparing for the journey to Frankfurt. She had sent on her luggage some days before, and Hans had told her that it arrived. That, she thought, was the final confirmation that she was leaving Paris. Tears came to her eyes while standing doing her make-up in front of the mirror in the bathroom.

But packing her suitcase that morning, she had ceased to think about that. It was after all, all settled. She'd soon be on the train to Frankfurt. She lied to the taxi-driver saying, Yes, going home for a few days. And at Gare d'Est, when he wished her a nice time, she didn't reply, and as she moved away, she heard herself say, Do you not see that I'm leaving Paris? And added, for ever.

Hans got dressed and lit a cigarette before going over to the baker's for some rolls. The morning was dry, but slightly overcast with hardly any wind blowing. The pigeons were cooing from the trees and the small birds singing in the garden hedges.

"Alle Vögel sind schon da...", all the birds are here already,

he hummed as he sauntered along the street to the

What Colette Didn't Know

kiosk for his newspaper and cigarettes. Gradually the clouds began to scatter and Hans felt the rays of the young sun warm on his back on his way back to the flat. What a change, he thought, this time last week, we had so much snow. He had sat on the sofa looking out at it. It only started snowing after he got up. But soon the streets and roofs were covered white. The snow, he thought, had quietened the birds too. Earlier, Hans heard them while it was still dark. Only the doves, nesting in the trees of the houses next door, continued their lonely coo-coo. If it's like this too in Paris,? Hans had wondered. He didn't know. He had only listened to the local weather report. The white flakes fell straight down, then suddenly were tossed in all directions by a squall of wind. From time to time the silence was broken by the sound of someone scraping snow from their windscreen. Hans was glad he didn't have to drive to work. I have my chauffeur, he thought, laughing. Here of course, he was referring to the tram. Besides, with this kind of weather, there will be traffic jams in the city. Hans laughed to himself again, And right in the middle of all that snow, the spring fashion in the shop windows seemed to make fun of it all.

Mike Crowley

Back in the flat Hans set about preparing breakfast. Today there was no rushing, so before setting the table, he put on a pot of coffee and fried two eggs with bacon and tomatoes. When all was ready, he sat down and began buttering the fresh rolls. The radio brought him up to date on world affairs, and the weather forecast announced that the clouds would disperse bringing sunny periods everywhere. Hans knew all that already, for now the sun was filling the room with its light, showing up the fine dust on the furniture that he had dusted down only the day before. Blast it, he cursed, where in the bloody hell does all this dust come from? Nice to hear the day will be nice, he said to himself, smiling with satisfaction and munching away, we'll have a sunshine welcome for Colette. He squirted a generous portion of mustard out of the tube, and now he was using what remained of the two rolls to clean off the plate. That done, and the plate almost as clean as when it was taken from the cupboard, Hans lit a cigarette, turned the radio off and got down to reading his newspaper.

The phone rang and Hans jumped up thinking it must be Colette. But no, it was only the office. It was a short call and when Hans hung up he return-

What Colette Didn't Know

ed to his newspaper. He glanced at his watch. Colette is well on her way now, he thought, lit another cigarette and continued reading. He was just doing the crossword when the phone rang a second time. Again the office. Yes, he said, he knew all about that and there would be time enough till Monday. He put back the receiver and going over to the table to get his cigarette he bragged, They can't get along without you, Hans, it's your fate to stay there for many more years. Then he sat down again, finished the crossword, folded the newspaper and threw it on the table. He switched on the TV, but the sun was shining on it so much that he had to go and draw the curtains. He sat down, lit a cigarette and began clicking through the programmes. Just as dull as the evenings, he grunted, and switched it off.

The flowers!, he said, bloody hell, the flowers!, suddenly remembering, that he had forgotten to buy some. Christ almighty, he cursed, pulling on his overcoat and racing off down the stairs, no flowers, that would never do! On his way to the flower shop he thought, Maybe I should go home again and get them at the railway station. But on second thoughts he said, It would be a warmer welcome with a vase of flowers on the table.

Mike Crowley

That's settled, he said to himself, entering the shop. Roses it would have to be, he said, looking round the place. On his way back the sun was hot as he sauntered along with his coat open and his bunch of roses.

When Hans came from the car park into the hall of the main station it was like entering a busy marketplace. The hall was teaming with people and Hans wondered where they all came from and where were they going. Some were pulling suitcases on wheels, others pushing trolleys full of luggage. Well-dressed men and women hurried along with their laptop hanging from their shoulder or carrying it in their hand. Teams of teenagers wearing jeans and sweatshirts with heavy rucksacks pushed their way through the crowd. There was more happening here, Hans thought, than in the city centre.

Lighting a cigarette he registered that the train from Paris would be five minutes late. Not bad at all, he said to himself, steering his way through the crowd to a bookshop. Inside everyone seemed oblivious of the hustle and bustle right outside the door. Most of the people that entered the shop just picked up a newspaper from the piles of national and foreign newspapers, paid and left. A few, like

What Colette Didn't Know

himself, just killing time thumbed through books and magazines. Hans did the same, wondering if he would have his manuscript ready for printing the beginning of the following year. Nervously he glanced at his watch, put the book back on the shelf and returned to the noisy railway hall. He lit a cigarette and crossed over to the platform where he stood waiting for the train.

In the flat Colette kicked off her shoes and went to the window. She pulled back the curtain, and went onto the balcony to have a look at her new surroundings. The small gardens in front of the houses were tidy and the hedges green. There were fir-trees in some of the gardens. The hedges running along the middle of the avenue were green too, but the trees were still bare with no signs of buds. It was a quiet street, Colette thought, no people and hardly any traffic.

This is a lovely street you're living in, she called to Hans, who, appearing from the kitchen, where he was preparing coffee said,

I'm glad you like it, Colette, It's a very nice place to live, and it's no distance from the centre. As well as that, we have very good public transport here.

Mike Crowley

While he talked, Hans put his cigarette into the ashtray on the table and went and stood beside Colette who was still looking out the window. He took Colette into his arms and kissed her.

Welcome to Frankfurt, he said, I hope you'll feel at home here.

They hugged and kissed, and then Hans took the cigarette and went back into the kitchen.

Coffee will be ready in a moment, he called out, I'll just have to lay the table.

Let me do that, Colette said, following him into the kitchen, Where do you keep the cups?

They had biscuits with the coffee. Colette said, She had sandwiches and coffee on the train, so she wasn't hungry. Hans suggested, they go for a pizza later in the evening.

What a huge flat you've got, Hans, she said, going around looking into the rooms.

Actually, it was a stroke of luck. I knew this fellow and after he got married, they decided to leave Germany and emigrate to Canada. He told me about the flat, because at that time I was in fact on the look out for one. Of course I wasn't thinking about something as big as this. But considering the matter, the rent and the area, I thought you can afford that Hans, you can always

What Colette Didn't Know

get rid of it later, if you find it too big.

A wonderful stroke of luck indeed, as you say, plenty of room for both of us.

That time, Colette, I never dreamed I'd be sharing it with you some day, he said, taking Colette in his arms and hugging her.

When I think of my small flat in Paris, Colette said.

Flats in Paris are expensive, as you often told me, he said.

Ah!, Paris, she sighed, just think of it, I was still there only ten hours ago.

Wait and see, my dear, you'll get to like Frankfurt yet, he said, trying to console her.

I suppose I will, Colette agreed, you get used to every place, somehow.

Oh, it's not going to be as bad as that, Colette, he said, when summer comes and you'll get to know the city, you'll simply love it here.

Hans lit a cigarette and Colette took the cups and things into the kitchen.

I'll do a bit of unpacking now, she said.

Whatever you like, Colette, he said, taking one of her cases into the bedroom, make yourself at home. Come, I'll show you where you can put your things.

Mike Crowley

Hans sat on the side of the bed watching Colette taking sweatshirts, underwear, jeans and jerseys and placing them in the wardrobe. She got out a pair of sandals and put them on.

For around the house, she said, smiling at Hans.

You'll have to register here, he said, we mustn't forget it.

Oh, yes, she said, can we go there tomorrow?

I suppose we could. Make sure you have your papers with you.

Good!, she said, first thing in the morning.

And the second thing tomorrow is to carry the cases to the basement, Hans added.

Okay!, Colette said, arranging her cosmetics in the bathroom.

And now, that you've got a bit organized, he said, we can be getting ourselves ready to go out.

The ticket system for trams and buses is more or less like in France, Hans explained, standing in front of the vending machine. You must first dial the number of where you want to go to. Then you press the kind of ticket you want, and when the price shows up on the display, you put the money in. I've a monthly ticket, but we have to get a ticket for you, Hans said, so dial number 50 and

What Colette Didn't Know

now put in the money. The tram was crammed. This is a bad time of day, Hans said, rush hour in the city, that's why we're crowded like sardines. But we haven't far to go. Hans had just finished talking when they had to get off again.

From here we'll take the U-Bahn to the Old Opera House, he said, I know a place there where they make very good pizze.

Outside the night air was crisp after the stuffy pizzeria.

Do you mind if we walk home, Colette,? this way you can get your first impression of Frankfurt.

If it's not too far, I'd like to see the shops.

Along the way Hans told Colette about the development of the city centre, and why Fressgasse was called Glutton lane. That Goethe Street was the most expensive street in town. Strolling along the shopping mile, Colette was interested in the shops and they went into some of the bigger stores, where they had a look at clothes and other things and all the time Hans kept on talking like a record telling Colette all about the street and the shops. Imagine, Hans said, The cars used to pass through here one time. But then

Mike Crowley

there were so many of them, that it was decided to close the street to traffic, and so they made a pedestrian zone out of it.

Back again at the centre, they went down to the ticket office and got a monthly ticket for Colette. In the tram on the way home, Hans explained, that her ticket was valid for travel on trams, busses and trains within the city boundary.

Chapter 10

Spring, that Colette was wishing for since last December while still in her Paris flat, was now, with each new day becoming more and more visible, and she believed she could even see the trees get greener and fuller while she looked on.

During the week when Hans was at the office, Colette would start out every morning discovering her new world. A new life in a new country with a new man. She would repeat this to herself looking at the street names and trying to remember them. As far as the new man was concerned, Colette thought, he wasn't really all that new anymore.

Mike Crowley

Each new day make him less new, she thought, and smiling to herself added, and in bed at night does the rest.

The first few weeks when Colette was still unfamiliar with her surroundings she usually took the tram or bus to and from town. A new life she would muse, seated in the tram looking out at the buildings, a new life will require more time.

Not long after her arrival in Frankfurt stepping off the tram one morning and the sun shining through the broken clouds, Colette's thoughts shot over to Paris. What would I be doing now, she asked herself, if I were still in Paris? A new life, she repeated, and am I not right in the middle of it,? she said to herself on her way to enrol at the City Library. And what's left now, Colette continued to herself, her eyes darting from one side of street to the other, what's left is a new country. Colette paused, stopping to look at the books on display in the library windows. This new country, she thought, was slowly beginning to lose its newness too. She knew the language and she was beginning to find her way round this city that would be her future home. And on weekends she had driven out with Hans to see parts of the surrounding countryside like Taunus and Rheingau.

What Colette Didn't Know

In the library Colette found a fairly good stock of books in her native language. Later she often popped in there to read the French newspapers. But the shops remained her greatest attraction.

She had plenty of time and so she could spend hours walking about in and out of the shops. In the big stores she went from floor to floor looking at everything on display. Sometimes she tried on some clothes wondering if she shouldn't buy something new for the summer. Hans had assured her that she could buy whatever she needed.

As the weeks went by it didn't take long for Colette to discover that the city was indeed in comparison with Paris very small and compact. Clothes shops and shoe shops, cosmetic shops, bakeries, jewellery shops, bookshops, delicatessen stores and spice shops were all only a stone's throw away from each other together with hair stylists, ice cream parlours, bars, cafés, fast food and cinemas. The big stores too had supermarkets in the basements.

Another attraction of hers was shopping at the open-air markets, where the farmers from the nearby countryside offered vegetables, potatoes, cheeses, butter, eggs, wine and even home-brewed beer. Colette also loved hanging round the covered market, locally called the Kleinmarkthalle. Here too, apart from local products, Colette found delicatessen and all sorts of fruits, vegetables and spices from all over the world, and that the whole year round.

As she got to know the city better, Colette ventured away from the shops and the centre down to the riverside. There she'd saunter along the banks of the Main with the skyscrapers of the financial district towering high above the city like some sort of gigantic cacti. Or she'd sit on a bench reading or watching the barges go by. Sometimes she'd cross the river to visit one of the many museums along the quay.

Further exploring her new home Colette wandered about in the parks. When the sun was shining she loved sitting outdoors, and she looked forward to the time when the cafés would put out their tables and chairs, and she could sit with a coffee like she used to do in Paris. The fountains too, scattered about the city, each with its own unique design, wouldn't be turned on till May.

Colette loved to cook, always wanting to prepare surprises for Hans when he'd come home from work. But though she told him she had all the time in the world for it, Hans very often in-

What Colette Didn't Know

sisted that they eat out. He always took her to a different restaurant. One evening to the Greeks, then to the Chinese or the Italians or they just went for a pizza. These evenings out were, of course no lavished dinners, but simply ordinary meals.

Whether at home or eating out, the love-birds were all the time engaged in lively conversations. Hans would rattle off how he had spent his day at work, each day more or less the same pattern with occasionally something new to report. Colette would talk in detail about where she went and what she discovered. And one such evening Colette surprised Hans telling him that she was now some weeks in Frankfurt, and that the only thing she could discover that Paris and Frankfurt had in common was, that the weather was more or less the same and that Frankfurt was just as cosmopolitan as Paris. In the end though, their conversations always finally turned to their upcoming marriage. The formalities were all settled, so there was nothing more in the way.

Chapter 11

They were still feeling tired when they arrived at Heraklion airport. The excitement of the last few days had sapped their energy, leaving them in need of a holiday. It was their honeymoon, and incidentally their first flight together since their meeting on the flight to Seoul, where it all began.

The marriage ceremony took place in Römer, the Town Hall. Outside the municipal building people went about their business, never bothering to consider what might be happening inside. Only a week before the square in front of the building

Mike Crowley

was crowded with people celebrating May Day. Colette's parents arrived the evening before the marriage and, together with Hans's brother, were the sole guests. Their daughter's marriage had all gone to quickly for them. When Colette broke the news during a one day visit to Colmar, where she introduced Hans to her parents, she noticed her father's cheeks redden. Colette could imagine what he was thinking, that Hans was old enough to be her father. But it was obvious, that Colette was in love with this man, from the way she spoke about him in the letters she sent home. His job too, it must be said, played an important part in the process of winning over her parents to accept Hans as their future son-in-law. At first Colette's mother thought there might be a grandchild on the way, but Colette scattered that thought, saying she wasn't pregnant. After the marriage the group had lunch at an Italian restaurant nearby, after which Colette's parents were taken to the train. Her parents had decided to return home that same evening, because Colette and Hans would be up early the next morning, so they would not see them again till after their honeymoon.

When Hans applied for holidays at short notice,

What Colette Didn't Know

Neuheimer turned it down. He knew that Hans had holidays coming to him, but he was only prepared to allow him one week off instead of the three weeks Hans wanted to get. Neuheimer reminded him that it was now almost six months since his trip to Seoul, and that Hans should arrange soon for a flight there to see how they're handling the project. Hans felt pleased and flattered with all that, but he still wanted the holidays, and finally they settled for a fortnight. Nobody knew that Hans was getting married, and that this was to be his honeymoon. Why Hans kept it to himself? Well, he himself couldn't account for his behaviour. He would, after all have to tell the company because of income tax matters and all that. His plan was to break the news to his staff over a glass of Sekt when he got back. The plan was carried out, but, as it turned, Hans was in no form for celebrating.

The transfer by bus from the airport to their hotel lead through Heraklion, giving them their first glimpse of the Cretan capital. Passing the famous archaeological museum they got a glimpse of the sea and the harbour as the bus picked its way through the cars that seemed to be getting in each other's way. Soon they lost sight of the sea speeding along the motorway, that looked very new, and was as straight as a rule. Again the sea came into sight, spread out like a blue plateau with the sun dancing on it. Colette and Hans hugged and kissed warming up to the holiday spirit. The sea came and went, sometimes hidden behind low hills till, the bus finally left the motorway and climbed to the top of a hill. Colette and Hans found themselves looking out onto an open countryside. There were houses in the distance and fields and olive trees and goats, and the sea was back again, more prominent than ever before.

Somewhere down there is our destination, I suppose, Hans remarked, straining his eyes to see if he could discover a hotel.

Further down the dusty road the view got better. Now there were people working in the fields, a donkey tied to a tree, dogs roamed about the houses, and then came the hotels and guest houses with swimming pools. In the distance there was something like a town, and further away a small harbour. At last the bus stopped outside a hotel, and the first passengers got off. Five minutes later, after climbing a bit of a hill, it came

What Colette Didn't Know

to a stop outside a big gateway with the name of their hotel written in big letters. It was a large compound surrounded by a wall. Colette and Hans, each pulling a suitcase, headed for the reception. Hans, who hadn't smoked since leaving the airport, lit a cigarette.

The apartments were dotted about the compound, all looking out to sea. Small tidy lawns with flowers and low shrubs decorated the entrances, with the house numbers clearly visible on the walls. Hans stumped out his cigarette in an ashtray on the table in front of the apartment. He opened the door, took Colette in his arms, and in they went. He then went and brought in the cases and locked the door.

Hans kicked off his sandals, jumped onto the spacious bed and said, Come here, Colette, we're on our honeymoon. Soon Colette was lying on top of him, her sandals too kicked into some corner of the room. Locked in each others arms Colette felt his prick pressing against her. Hans released himself from her, pulled off his clothes, and flung them from him. Colette too pulled off her T-shirt, but before she could strip further, Hans took her and rolled over onto her. He pulled off her bra, and while they caressed madly, his hand moved down her body and undid the remaining obstacle. Colette sighed clinging onto Hans, his hands wrapped round her bottom, his cock hard against her belly. Kissing and licking, tight in each other's embrace, Colette let go her hand, took hold of his cock and pushed it into her. She moaned and sighed as Hans put on the pressure, giving her the works. He sucked her nipples, then went back to her lips, groaning on his way to a crescendo. Colette too groaned and wriggled, and he felt her tighten round his cock the moment his juice gushed into her. That was some fuck, he thought, panting, trying to get back his breath. Some moments later he rolled off Colette and lay on his back. Colette found his hand, and together they remained panting, looking up at the ceiling.

When his heart got back to normal, Hans released his hand, kissed Colette and got up. He took a cigarette from the packet he had thrown on the table, lit it and went and opened the veranda door. The air that came in was fresh and fragrant. Hans remained at the door looking out to sea. He could smell his own sweat, as if he hadn't washed in weeks. Colette watched him from the bed, wondering what he might be thinking. Neither of them spoke. When he finished smoking, Hans

What Colette Didn't Know

looked round for an ashtray and found one on the table. He crushed the butt into it. And now for a shower, he said to Colette, making off for the bathroom. Colette heard the water and Hans moaning as if he were having another orgasm.

It's fantastic, he called out to Colette, could you bring me the shampoo, honey? Hans didn't have to call a second time, for Colette was up like a shot, and after digging in her suitcase, came in with the plastic bottle, and joined him under the shower. The hot shower was invigorating after the journey, and the two soaped and rubbed each other down. They kissed, and clung to each other, and Hans thought of going to bed again, but Colette caught his cock and began manipulating it. When she brought him to boiling point, the juice gushed into her hand, but was quickly washed away in the water. Hans held her close, while she played with his balls.

After drying themselves, Hans lit a cigarette and began unpacking. Colette took the clothes, and hung them in the wardrobe with her own. They drank the last of the water they had with them, and realized that they were slowly getting hungry. Hans pulled on a pair of boxers, Bermuda shorts that he had picked up at a sale, and a loose

Mike Crowley

T-shirt, and slipped into a pair of sandals. He crushed the butt in the ashtray, and watched Colette looking at herself in the mirror in her cotton slacks and T-shirt. After getting into her sandals, she posed again, looking at her wedding ring, and smiling at Hans. Hans put the flight tickets and other valuables into the safe, and hung the key around his neck. Colette closed the veranda door, packed their swimming gear into a small rucksack, locked the door behind them and set out to explore their surroundings.

Colette was sure she had never any leaning towards becoming a writer, so she was very surprised when she discovered a diary hidden away in the lower draw of a press while sorting out her things before leaving for Frankfurt. Sitting on the side of her bed, reading through it, she could hardly believe she had written what she found there. The handwriting wasn't as developed as her present handwriting, but she agreed nonetheless, that there was indeed a similarity, which convinced her, take it or leave it, that she had written it. And the names here, she thought, paging through it, these names don't ring a bell, they must be nicknames for some of her school-

What Colette Didn't Know

mates. Amused by her discovery, Colette decided she would begin keeping a diary when she gets to Frankfurt.

The diary was in French. Colette told herself that her native language was French, and therefore she was entitled to write in that language. And she added, again to herself, It wasn't to hide anything from Hans. In fact, she didn't mention anything about it to him, content with the fact, that it was no concern of his anyway. In the first pages Colette points out very clearly, that there are no secrets between herself and Hans. Hans, she wrote, tells her everything, especially all about what happens at work. She wrote too, that, if she marries Hans, she would have to get a job doing something, though Hans had already told her, she would not have to work. But she told him, she would not know how to fill in her days, she had no special hobbies like writing, painting, or something of the sort, that would help keep her occupied. She was young, and if she at least got work for say ten to fifteen years, after which time, Hans would be pensioned off anyway, she too could stop working, and they could both enjoy life, even going away for longer periods. Her diary was not to be a day-to-day account of what happened, she would keep it only to note down something special, including thoughts she might regard as worth recording. She took the diary along to Crete with her.

Their honeymoon was to be a lazy holiday with no set plan. They got up late in the mornings, prolonged their breakfast drinking coffee, after which they collected their swimming gear and set out for the beach. The compound had its own private beach, but Colette and Hans preferred the public beach. To get there they had to leave the compound and trot off down the narrow streets, where small shops offered everything from beach gear to souvenirs, postcards and paperbacks in several languages, and cigarettes. Hans had even turned to smoking Papastratos, and took two cartons back to Frankfurt.

At the beach they lounged about in the Cretan sun, chatting, reading, from time to time venturing into the water for a dip, or sitting enjoying a chilled beer or a Greek coffee at one of the taverns that lined the beach. But they did however manage to get away on a few occasions, and their first visit was to Knossos.

It was a conducted tour and they were picked

What Colette Didn't Know

up right outside the compound. The entrance to this great site of Cretan civilization was chock-a-block with cars and buses, and French, English, German, and goodness knows what other languages, summed in the air like bees in a hive. Making their way through the palace, the group had to stay close together, to hear what the guide was saying, and to make sure not to get lost. But they survived it, and later the group was taken by bus to a nearby town, where they had lunch.

The trip to the Samaria gorge was quite a different story. Colette found out about it in a long list of sites of interest hanging on a wall beside the reception. Enquiring at the desk, she was told, that it was a nature reserve with a hiking trail of about fifteen kilometres. To hike the whole way you needed good footwear, because parts of it can be difficult and even dangerous. When Hans heard that, he said, Well, that's out for us, Colette, with our sandals, we'd probably never make it.

But we could hire a car and drive down there for a picnic, Colette suggested.

Good idea, Colette, your word is my command.

The gorge turned out to be a sanctuary of silence. It was still early in the day, and, though the sky

Mike Crowley

was blue with no sign of clouds, it was chilly up there. Except for the birds chirping and people's voices coming from somewhere down below in the gorge, there wasn't a sound anywhere. The hikers, Hans said, must have started out early, because now, apart from a few tourists, they had the place to themselves. There were notices prohibiting visitors to leave the marked out paths, and Hans had to keep his smokes in his pocket, because smoking was strictly forbidden as well. As the morning went by and the sun got warmer, they looked round for a nook where they could enjoy their picnic. The tables and benches, which were attached to them, were made of wood. Getting through souvlaki, salad, potatoes, olives and white bread with water to wash it down, Colette went off into raptures about their visit to Heraklion some days before and the fantastic display of food in the markets there. It would be great if they could go there at least one more time. When they left the gorge, before going home, they had coffee at a nearby tavern.

Travelling to Heraklion meant that Colette and Hans had to be up earlier than usual, in order not to miss the bus. The day again was promising with

What Colette Didn't Know

the sun shining in a blue sky, though there were some patches of cloud far out over the sea. It was cloudy too in the capital. Getting off the bus outside the museum, Colette, glancing at the sky, said, it might even rain. Doubt it, Hans said, if anything it will rain out at sea. He lit a cigarette and sent Colette to get tickets for the museum. Hans remarked, It would take days to get round the museum, if you wanted to see it properly. By the time they were out again, it was midday. The sun shone in a turquoise sky with no trace of a cloud. After finishing the water they had brought with them and having a coffee at the museum, Colette and Hans set out for a place to eat.

They went off in the direction of downtown, Hans having to stop at every jeweller's shop for Colette to have a look at the array of dazzling golden rings, chains and bracelets. Sauntering through the market area Hans, a cigarette hanging from his lips and holding Colette's hand, amused himself listening to her talking excitedly about everything she saw. There were all kinds of fresh fish spread out on stone counters, piles of fruits and vegetables of all sorts, bottles of olive oil, olives prepared in jars, herbs, spices and flowers filling the air with their fragrance, and tourists.

Mike Crowley

They walked about looking at and talking about everything they saw, and taking photos.

Not a table vacant, Colette said, looking around, the tourists are all over the place, both inside and outside the restaurants.
Yeah, Hans said, It doesn't look as if it's going to be easy to find a table.
He lit a cigarette, for he was getting a little nervous with all those people. They turned and walked back the way they came, their eyes searching every corner for a vacant seat. All Heraklion must be gathered here, Hans remarked, we seem to have bad cards today. But just then Colette said, Over there, lets go quickly before it's gone.
Colette and Hans were glad to be sitting outside, because inside it sounded very noisy. Waiters racing about, tourists and natives munching all kinds of delicacies, and all talking loudly. Colette went in to the toilet. When she came back, she told Hans the kitchen was visible for all to see. There was fish on a grill over a charcoal fire and huge pots steaming on a stove. The cooks were busy preparing the menus and in one corner of the kitchen there was a woman

What Colette Didn't Know

scrubbing pots over a huge sink.

Colette, studying the menu, said she could eat everything on it, that one dish was more scrumptious than the other. Hans agreed, but added that even if they tried, they couldn't get through it in one day.

Ha, ha, Colette said, then we'll have to come here more often.
Maybe!, he replied.

They settled for grilled sardines, broccoli, fried potatoes and a jug of local wine. Bread they didn't have to order, it was served up anyway. It was delicious, and Colette said, She could go on eating forever. When they were finished, Hans lit a cigarette and went to the toilet. When he came out, he remarked, that inside the restaurant there was more garlic than oxygen in the air.

Colette laughed, and asked, Since when, Hans, have you anything against garlic?
Hans ignored the remark and said, How about a coffee now, Colette?
I think the wine has gone to my head, she said, rubbing her hand across her forehead.

Mike Crowley

Well, the coffee is the right man for that, Hans said.

Inside the coffee house there were only men sitting around tables drinking coffee, some reading the newspaper and others playing dominoes. Colette and Hans took a seat outside. Colette ordered coffee and Hans had a Greek coffee and two uosos. Hans lit a cigarette and poured some water into the uosos. It was pleasant sitting in the shade watching the people pass by, gesticulating, pointing out this thing or that, stopping to take a photo, all from different nations. When they called the waiter to pay, he told them in German that the uoso was on the house. He said, He worked in a hotel in Frankfurt where he learned his German. They thanked the waiter and walked back to the bus stop for their bus home.

Hans kept his word to Colette in the Samaria gorge, so the last day before returning to Frankfurt, they went again to Heraklion. When they got off the bus at the museum, they strolled down to the harbour, and from there up through the narrow streets leading to the city centre. The sun was hot like in summer, though it was still

What Colette Didn't Know

only May. The streets were very quiet with no traffic, but cars parked bumper to bumper on both sides of the street. Colette and Hans stopped to look back at the harbour and the sea. Hans lit a cigarette as they turned and walked off again wondering how to get out as if caught in a labyrinth. The buildings looked like offices, and nobody around to ask the way. They hadn't a clue where they were or in what part of the town they'd come out, but, rounding a corner, they found themselves right in the market place where they were the first time. All roads lead to Rome, they said, together. All was well again, for here they knew their way around.

Lets have a drink, Colette said, I feel like I'm almost dehydrated
They drank beer and Hans had a smoke. Colette went to a nearby stand and returned with postcards and wrote them while having her drink.
On the way back to the bus, they walked past the same shops they had seen on their first visit to the capital, but still, Colette couldn't pass the jewellery shops without stopping to look. At one of the shops, Hans noticed that Colette seemed to be interested in the bracelets.

Will we go in and have a look round?, he sug-

gested, looking into Colette's eyes.
Colette smiled, and as she turned to go in, Hans glanced up and down the street, dropped the cigarette onto the pavement, and stood on it. A sales-woman came over to them and asked if she could help. Colette, seeing the badge on the woman's blouse, began speaking French. Both women smiled, and chatted away as they walked to the counter. The woman took a tray of bracelets from a drawer and Colette beckoned to Hans to come over. Colette pointed out a bracelet, and the woman tied it round her wrist. Colette looked at it, then looked at Hans, standing there beside her not understanding a word.

Beautiful, she said, isn't it, posing with the bracelet.

Yes, indeed, Hans said, it suits you down to the ground.

Still admiring it, she told Hans the price.

If you like it, Colette, never mind the price, it's our honeymoon.

Colette smiled again.

The woman took the bracelet from Colette's wrist, took the price tag off, and put it into a small cloth bag. Outside Colette threw her arms round

What Colette Didn't Know

his neck.
Oh, Hans, thank you very much, she said.
Before getting on the bus, Hans lit a cigarette while he listened to Colette telling him that the woman in the shop had lived in Paris for some time.
Next day they had already left Crete on their flight home, when Hans thought about the company for the first time since the holidays. Amazing, he said to himself, this must have something to do with marriage and Colette. In one or two weeks he'd be off to Paris, and then sometime later on a trip to Seoul. He considered taking Colette with him, but he decided not to mention anything in case it mightn't work out and she'd be disappointed.

Chapter 12

The bad news on his desk the day after his honeymoon vacation had shattered Hans. His plan was to call his office staff together that morning and watch their reaction to the news of his marriage. He would still have to go on with this plan, but now it wouldn't be the same thing because he really felt lousy. And he was in such good form before going to work, joking with Colette at breakfast, telling her all about his plan, and what a pity it was she couldn't be there too to watch the staff's reaction. I'll have it all for you tonight, Colette, I'm sure it will be amusing. The

weather was okay too. Dry and sunny, though not at all as warm as Crete. But the trees and bushes had thrived during his absence. Well, after all, Hans said to himself, we're well into May.
Hans got up from his desk and went and opened the door of the adjoining office. He called his secretary in and returned to his desk. He sat down and lit a cigarette.

Please sit down, he said, looking down on the desk like someone arranging his thoughts.

Mrs Neuss sat down and put her writing-pad and biro on the desk. Standing up again, she went to the window saying, I'll draw the blinds, boss, it's too sunny here, and returned to her chair. Hans said nothing. He finished his cigarette, crushed the butt in the ashtray and looked up at Mrs Neuss.

Yeah, it's very sunny this morning, he began, and went on, Mrs Neuss, I want you to order Sekt and some titbits for the office. We're going to have a party during the midday break.

Mrs Neuss was used to this stuff, but today she didn't like the look of the boss's face. He was all smiles when he came in that morning but now… She wrote down the order with date and time.

Oh!, and a couple of bottles of water and fruit

What Colette Didn't Know

juice as well, he added.
Okay, boss. Anything else?
Is there coffee for the nine o'clock meeting?
I'll look after it, she said.

As soon as word got out that Mr Konrad was throwing a party, speculation started mounting. His birthday wasn't till later in the year. Did Mrs Neuss not ask him what's up? No!. Funny, she usually knows everything. How long is he in the company? Could it be an anniversary? No, that's not it either, Mrs Neuss would certainly know that. Promotion! That's it! Our boss is promoted!

When the staff went into the conference-room, they looked hard at Hans, trying and hoping to discover something in his face. He sat at the head of the table his arms resting on a pile of papers, waiting for the staff to sit down. Mrs Neuss poured coffee for Hans and the others followed suit, helping themselves from the coffeepots placed along the table. Hans looked round at the faces looking at him, their writing-pads open and biros in hand ready to take notes.

Before I went on holidays, Hans began, I was of two minds, whether to tell you then, or to wait

till after my holiday.
The eyes glued on him opened wider.
 Well, as you can see, I waited.
He paused and again looked round at the faces staring back at him, this time more inquisitively.

 I got married, he said, grinning.
There was a moment's silence, as if Hans had told them something unbelievable, and some thought, relaxing, and settling themselves in their chairs, Hans was not the boss they knew. Hans relaxed too, and beaming all over told them they were the first to hear about his marriage. Not even the personal office knows anything yet. He then mentioned the party and got on with the meeting.

By week's end all his talks with the personal office were to no avail, and Hans would have to go by the end of June. Now that the matter was cleared, Neuheimer called a staff meeting the following week, and informed them that Mr Konrad would be leaving the company the end of June. Of course, nobody asked any questions, and Neuheimer didn't elaborate. Hans wasn't present at the meeting.
Back in the office, the staff wondered as to what

What Colette Didn't Know

might have happened.
"Mr Konrad just got married," said one, "how come that he's leaving the company?"
"Maybe she's a millionairess," said another.
"Ah, nonsense," said another, "just married and he quits the job. And at his age?"
"That's not like Konrad," someone else butted in, "he always acted as if he were married to the job."
"Ha, ha," cawed another, "now he's got a wife."
"Fired, I tell you," said someone else, "Konrad didn't quit of his own."
"You might have a point there," said another, "Konrad wouldn't throw up the job at his age, and besides, if he did for some reason whatsoever, then he'd have showed up at the meeting, and we'd have Neuheimer regretting, that our dear colleague, Mr Konrad will be leaving us the end of the month."

The group broke up returning to their desks, with more questions open than answered.

Business was as usual in the few weeks left. Hans didn't mention anything about his dismissal to anyone, and no one asked him any questions. And once or twice when Neuheimer came and said, Hans, we'll have to get together this afternoon to discuss this or that, Hans refused saying,

Mike Crowley

You'll probably get along all right without me, or have you not heard, that I'll be gone the end of the month. Sarcastic bastard, Neuheimer thought, but he also knew that Hans was insulted and furious. So Hans Konrad came and went as he pleased and didn't give a damn about the lot.

Some days later Hans went along to the labour exchange. There they told him to come back when he had all his personal documents together and they handed him a list of the required documents, adding that he might also check the job offers in the newspapers.

This advice he took in fact, and as he slowly recovered from the shock and plucked up some courage, he admitted to himself, that he was after all only in his mid-fifties, not by any means fit for the scrap heap. So he turned to studying the job offers in the weekend papers in the hope that he would find a job and so just glide from the company into a new job. The fact that Colette was looking through the adds as well, made it all the more easier for Hans. So it seemed to cause no suspicion when Hans, reading the adds would say, I'll just have a look at the adds to see if there is anything of interest for you, Colette. If he came

What Colette Didn't Know

across anything for himself, he took the page and put it into his briefcase for further examination on Monday, when he'd be out of the house, and on his own. Offers there were, but soon his applications came back one after the other with all the apologies in the world, and it became clear to Hans, that his chances of getting work were very slim, even hopeless. His references were excellent, but his age was the obstacle. Again my age, he shouted, every time he read another rejection. God almighty, I'm only fifty-five!, what the hell has my age got to do with it? I'm sick of reading in the papers that some bastard or other is about to begin a new career at seventy or even eighty years of age, with one leg in the grave.

Finally the day came when Hans Konrad was no longer department manager in a company of good standing, but an unemployed man struggling with the alarm clock as to whether to get up or stay in bed. It was a matter of keeping up appearances. The first few weeks were the worst. Hans stretched out in the bed and cursed the company. Ah!, he said to himself, I'm a free man now and I can get up or stay in bed as long as I want. They can all go to hell with their meetings and charts and statistics and all that shit. I'm finished with it all and no loss. Long live freedom! Colette's sleepy voice would then announce, Hans, I think I heard the alarm.

Yes, yes, Colette, I turned it off. If you remember, I told you, I'll go in later in future. I'm serious about cutting down my overtime.
But make sure you don't fall asleep again, or you might be too late.
Never mind, Colette, like I told you, that doesn't interest me much anymore.
Colette said no more and Hans got up. When he returned from the bathroom, Colette was up as every morning preparing breakfast, while Hans was dressing. After breakfast Hans got ready to go and after planking a kiss on Colette's unwashed cheek, he took his briefcase and left.

Walking to the tram stop every morning, Hans found it hard to try and keep up appearances, especially during the first few weeks he had the impression that he didn't walk like when he was working, somehow he felt he was lacking in spirit. And how glad he was it was Summer, because

What Colette Didn't Know

now he would have to find a way of passing the time. He'd straighten himself up as he approached the kiosk where he got his morning newspaper.

"Taking a later tram this morning?," the woman remarked, laughing, giving him the change.

At work Neuheimer read a more serious paper and exchanged it later with Hans for his tabloid. The same people were waiting for the tram as every morning. Hans straightened himself again, for he felt he was sagging. I wonder do they recognize that I'm idle?, Hans thought looking cautiously around him to see if he couldn't detect anything in the way the bystanders acted or looked at him. The tram arrived and during the short run to the centre nothing unusual happened.

Hans observed from the determined way the people walked that they knew where they were going and that they were set on getting there quickly. He had about five minutes to wait for his commuter. He could in fact have taken any commuter as far as the main station, and change there, but Hans decided to wait. You never know, he told himself, maybe someone might notice me not taking my usual commuter and get suspicious.

Mike Crowley

But on second thoughts, well, of course I could be going somewhere else on business. If I took the airport commuter for example, people would probably say, that fellow is going away on business. He's probably some kind of top manager. But another thought would strike him and he'd half smile at the idea. What if the people standing around are in the same situation as himself? Again great stuff for a book, he chuckled, delighted with the idea.

One morning a young good looking woman caught his eye interrupting his train of thought. What the devil is she looking at me like that for? Hans asked himself. Has she perhaps discovered me? He took a small mirror about the size of a matchbox from his pocket and checked his face and hair. Vanity of vanities, he muttered and put the mirror back into his pocket. When he looked up again, the woman was gone. That too would be a good idea for a story, he went on again taking up his train of thoughts.

I have all the time in the world now, and supposing I choose to follow one of these people to see if they are just like me pretending to be going to work? One or two, or indeed all of them might be out of work too. Of course I'd have to

What Colette Didn't Know

play it very carefully. But I won't start today, he'd say to himself, I've time. And even if they did notice me walking after them, they would probably think that I too must be working somewhere around, maybe even in the same company as themselves.

Another morning when Hans got on the commuter he took a seat beside a fat man wearing glasses. The man sat with his newspaper spread out, his arm resting on the windowsill. He turned and smiled at Hans as he pulled in a bit in his seat to make room for Hans. On reaching the central station Hans got off and took the escalator to the main hall. There he went into a café.

He took a seat in the far off corner where he had a good view of everything that was happening. He ordered a coffee. He would in fact have preferred something stronger, but he knew there was no chance before ten. Well, he knew one or two places outside of the station that were open from six on, but that might be a little risky, he thought. Somebody might know him there and be surprised meeting him there at that hour of the morning. He also decided against reading the newspaper till later. The hustle and bustle around him kept Hans busy enough. He thought too that

Mike Crowley

he knew now why all the great authors spend so much time lounging about in cafés. And I like a bloody fool stuck inside that firm for the past thirty years. Is it any wonder then that I can't write? He glanced at his watch every now and then like a person making sure not to miss the train or maybe an appointment. An old fellow in the corner with unwashed hair and certainly not the cleanest of clothes looked up from his paper and stared over at Hans. Hans looked away pretending he hadn't noticed anything. That fellow's probably idle, Hans thought, I wonder if he thinks the same about me? I must get out of here. He glanced at his watch again. Waiter, he called and paid.

Outside more and more people were rushing about with briefcases and suitcases and rucksacks. It's safe enough now, Hans thought, nine o'clock, they're all at work by now. I'll go to the airport where I can sit around and read my paper in peace. In fact the trip to the airport didn't cost him anything, for he had a monthly ticket paid by the company which was also valid for the airport. Blast them, he thought, I have at least that out of the devils.

At the airport Hans hurried to the supermarket

What Colette Didn't Know

where he got a small bottle of Schnaps. He then went to the Gents and drank half the bottle. He felt better after that and he could even feel himself straightening up as the spirits wandered through his bloodstream. After finding a seat in the departures hall he got out his paper. Ah, the bastards, he said reading the headlines half loud, The government has further plans to boost the economy as exports continue to soar.

Chapter 13

What is it Hans? You look pale, Colette asked looking anxiously at him as they sat having breakfast.

Why do you ask,? Hans said, staring a little surprised at Colette.

Oh, nothing. Like I said, I just thought you look a little pale this morning.

Ah, so,? A little bit pale,? Hans said putting on a weak smile, probably because I didn't sleep so well last night.

Then it's not so bad, you can make up for that tonight. And do try and get out of work early.

Mike Crowley

I will, Colette, I'll try.
To himself Hans thought, That's the labour exchange. It's taking an effect on me before I even go there. But now there's no turning back. His papers had finally arrived from the company the day before.

The large envelope contained a reference, tax card and an accompanying letter wishing him all the best for his future. So that's it, Hans said, after reading the letter and checking through the papers, now I have nothing more to do with the place. That's the end of it, and that the whole thing should have happened in a matter of months. There is no justice in the world. Hans Konrad unemployed! And now I've got no other choice but to go along to that cursed labour exchange. Hans sorted out the papers he needed and put them into his briefcase. I suppose I'd better go there tomorrow. In that way I'll get it over and done with, and besides it will give me something to do other than having to go to the airport or somewhere else.

Hans put the rest of the papers away and took his briefcase to the table in the hall. Then he went into the living-room, threw himself onto the sofa

What Colette Didn't Know

and picked up a book from the table. Not a matter for suicide yet, he thought, though it mightn't have been a bad idea at all that I began thinking about it. He dropped the book and looked at the cigarette smouldering in the ashtray.

My god, I wonder what they're going to say to me at the labour exchange? There, they'll probably say when I leave the office, "Another idler, another one that doesn't want to work." But then half seriously half jokingly one of them will remark, "Ah well, as long as those types are around, we won't be out of a job." At that they'll all laugh, as if they had heard it for the first time, and one of them will get up, open the door and say: "The next please". Hans paused, took the cigarette and inhaled deeply. While the smoke escaped through his nose Hans nodded and said to the empty room, Yes, that's the way things go.

The following morning Hans was rushing around as usual as if getting ready for work, and after straightening his tie in front of the mirror in the hall, took his briefcase and said, Bye, Colette, see you this evening. Outside on the street Hans said looking up at the sky, What beautiful weather we have. Who'd want to go working on a day like

Mike Crowley

this? The end of July already. Imagine, it took them all that time to send me the papers. At the traffic lights he hesitated whether to cross over and take the tram or maybe he should walk. Many people walked during the good weather, so there would be nothing suspicious about it if he did the same. So he decided to walk. I have time enough, he thought, and if I walk on slowly, I'll be there around nine o'clock. That's early enough.

All the time Hans did his best to show a determined attitude like the people walking in front of him. He was just at the traffic lights when a young fellow ran across, though it was red.

Well, well, Hans said, turning to the people standing there, we're all in a hurry to get to work, but we don't have to get ourselves knocked down by a car getting there.

You said it, one man answered, the job isn't going to run away.

You can bet on that, Hans said.

Laughing they wished each other a pleasant day at work and walked on.

Hans, a little carried away with himself, suddenly realized that he was walking too fast.

What Colette Didn't Know

Slow down, Hans, he said to himself, you're going nowhere, and he steadied his pace. That fellow and his pleasant day. Have a pleasant day at work. Have a pleasant day at the labour exchange. Easy for them talking like that. This week they'll have their monthly salary on their bank account. Careful now, I'll have to watch out that nobody sees me turning in here. He glanced around him and putting on more speed, he said, All's clear, let's get going, and standing as erect as he could he walked into the building.

The people around probably think I'm working here, he consoled himself. Since his first visit there some two months before, Hans knew where to go. He took a number from the machine and sat waiting his turn with the others. Hans thought it took ages. The people sat holding their papers in envelopes or plastic bags. Every time someone came in, Hans got nervous and tried to see who it was without turning his head. When at last his turn came, he got up and very professional like took his briefcase and went into the office.

Every time Hans went to the airport, he knew he was taking a great risk. There was always the danger of meeting someone, he didn't want to meet. But with a valid ticket for the airport, Hans was prepared to take the risk, because it was nonetheless a good place to hide for part of the day. All this was during the first few weeks, when Hans really felt like a fish out of water. The thirty years of routine living had fallen apart, leaving Hans suspended. On the other hand, staying around the city was much more risky. So, considering the pros and cons, it was with a certain apprehension that Hans put the papers back into his briefcase and left the labour exchange for the airport. Because he was still on the company's payroll, and would be till the end of the year, they told him at the labour exchange, that he was not entitled to dole money, and handing him his papers said, he should come back with the papers in October or November.

Hans, his briefcase resting on his knees, looked out of the window of the train at the sun shining in a cloudless blue sky. Pity to be in here, he thought, a day like this, how I'd much prefer to be out rambling along by the river or wandering through the woods instead of sitting around in the airport. Indeed, Hans might have settled for the one or the other, but he had to admit, that he might look very foolish sauntering along dressed in a suit and tie and carrying a briefcase a glorious day like this. Crazy, he thought, laughing.

Hans was standing in the hall looking up at the arrival board, pondering over the flights from the different cities, when a voice behind him almost startled him.

Well, well, Mr Konrad, he heard, turning round and automatically taking the outstretched hand, I never dreamed of seeing you so soon again.

Hallo Mr Breul, Hans said, feeling his face getting hot and adding, me too Mr Breul, seems we're all circling in narrow spaces.

True, true, Mr Konrad, he said, still holding onto Hans's hand. And tell me, Mr Konrad, are you travelling yourself or collecting someone?

Collecting someone, Mr Breul, I was just checking out the schedule.

Indeed, Mr Konrad, I noticed that when I spotted you.

Mr. Breul was a client of the company where Hans used to work. Both men met couple of times a year over many years, so they knew each other very well.

You know, said Mr Breul, placing an arm round Hans's shoulder and steering him aside out of the people's way, when I heard about you leaving the company, I said, that can only mean that Mr Konrad has found a better position somewhere else. Would I be right, Mr Konrad?

Hans, feeling somewhat trapped, looked at Mr Breul wondering how to answer. But Breul, not waiting for an answer, followed up with another question that almost bowled Hans over.

And where my dear Mr Konrad is that better position? Hans swallowed and looked Breul in the eyes. The state, Mr Breul, he said, the civil service.

Didn't I know it, Breul said, bursting out laughing and clapping Hans on the back, didn't I know I was right. Hans was of course referring to the labour exchange as his employer, though he was not as yet getting money from them.

No better employer, Mr Konrad, you can now sit out your time till retirement without any worries. I'm sure even as a state employee you can go into retirement earlier than the rest of us taxpayers.

Hans, feeling cornered by all these questions said, Yes, I think so, something like that all right.

Sure, Mr Konrad, Breul went on laughing, as if it were all a joke, all very complicated, I'm sure.

Indeed, Mr Breul, twill take me all my time till retirement until I've learned all the paragraphs and regulations.

I've no doubt, it will, Mr Konrad, but you won't notice the time passing. Comfortable position. No worries, no stress.

Breul glanced at his watch, Must be off, Mr Konrad, my flight is due to leave in just under an hour. Shaking hands, Hans said, Nice to have met you, Mr Breul, and have a pleasant flight.

My pleasure, Mr Konrad, and again laughing loudly, don't overwork yourself, old man.

No danger about that, Hans called after him, watching him till he was out of sight.

Whee, Hans made looking round him, releasing the pent up feeling that almost smothered him. Oh, shit!, he cursed, taking a cigarette out of the packet, no smoking here, as he followed the sign to smokers corner. There he lit up and sank into the seat letting his head fall back against the seatback, his briefcase clamped between his knees. He was exhausted. When he finished smoking, he felt better. He pulled himself upright and turned his head in the direction of the ashtray beside him where he deposited the butt. Must go and eat something, he said to himself taking his briefcase and getting to his feet.

In the Schwarzwald Hans sat at the bar and

ordered a beer and a sandwich. There's something for Breul to chew on, Hans said to himself, taking a long drink from his glass. But out here you're skating on thin ice, he told himself. Wouldn't I love to see Neuheimer's face when he gets to hear the news."You did, Mr Breul…? At the airport…? With the civil service, you say? Well, that's something for you. Never thought Konrad would end up there. And at his age too. He's nearly better off than ourselves, Mr Breul."
"Maybe we ought to think about it, Mr Neuheimer, times are getting harder, even for us."

It seems that neither Neuheimer nor any of those that knew that Hans was fired, ever mentioned it to anyone, not even to clients. Must see if I still have his phone number, Mr Breul, Neuheimer would say, must give him a ring sometime. Hans eat the sandwich and washed it down with the rest of the beer, then took his briefcase and went to catch a commuter to the city. Opening the door to his flat Hans thought, Breul would believe anything.

The summer dragged on into September and Hans was feeling sick and tired of his miserable, even deplorable situation, the rejected applications

What Colette Didn't Know

with the sarcastic remarks about his age. Colette hadn't found work and she spent a lot of her time exploring the city. All this was a big problem for Hans, because Colette was liable to show up anywhere in town. Hans had to avoid places like the public library, parks, museums, art galleries and big stores, making it extremely difficult for him to find a safe hiding place. It was a headache every morning when he left the house, wondering where to go and how to pass the day. At times he felt like a man on the run. But when he returned home one evening it was with mixed feelings that he received the news from Colette weaving a letter in front of his eyes.

A letter from the airport, Hansy.
Hans smiled at her staring into her beaming eyes. He knew Colette wanted to get work, and he also knew that she wanted to continue flying.

And guess what,? she teased, I have work, Hansy, a job at the airport.

Great news, Colette, he said, if you'll just give me a little time to digest it.
Hans knew he hadn't said the right thing, and throwing his briefcase into his room, he thought, Colette at the airport.? So that's out, no more airport for me. Can't go there anymore.

Mike Crowley

It's shift work, Colette told him, one week early, one week late. No nights.
In some respect this was good news, but it too had its problems for Hans. My situation is still precarious, he told himself.

When Colette had early shift, she was up and out of the house before Hans got up. During that week, Hans could stay in bed as long as he liked, and he didn't have to leave the house till around midday. With late shift it was a horse of a different colour. That week he would have to get away early, but he could return home in the early afternoon. Both shifts had advantages, he agreed, but he had to remain watchful. Take, for example that time in July, when Hans sat reading the newspaper in the hope of finding work, and out of the blue Colette says, What about the Paris office, Hans?

Why Colette, what about it?

In Crete you told me you'd be going there shortly after our return.

Oh!, he said, smiling, laying the newspaper aside, did I not tell you, I've appointed someone else to do that? I don't have to go to Paris when you're here, Colette, he said, laughing.

Colette smiled, but added, and Seoul? Is that

What Colette Didn't Know

still on?

Seoul is out too, my dear, I told them I was too busy for the trip this time. But to be frank with you, Colette, the truth is, that I wanted to take you along with me, but this was turned down. Staff only, you know how it is, Colette, insurance and all that.

But Hans, she sighed, you never said a word about it till…

Well, now you know it, Colette.

Hans was glad that Colette had swallowed the story. On another occasion Colette brought up the topic of holidays, but with her new job, that matter could be squashed for the time being.

Chapter 14

Hans took a seat in the shade. He had in fact no great choice, because all the other benches in the park were occupied by sunbathers, enjoying the Indian summer. Hans too was delighted with the weather, the only thing about it being that it was too hot for walking.

He left the house in the early afternoon, to be out of the way before Colette returned from her early shift at the airport. With a cigarette between his lips and his briefcase, Hans strolled along wondering which way to take. In his briefcase he had a book and the newspaper which he had read

Mike Crowley

already that morning. Hot, he said to himself, too hot to go anywhere far away. His mind suggested the library, but Hans rejected it off hand. Not on a day like today, he told himself, too stuffy in there in this kind of weather. A glorious day indeed it was with the people going about wearing light clothes as in summer. Walking past a park Hans remarked to himself, Indian summer or not, the few leaves left on the trees had long ago turned to bronze. He stopped walking, turned back and went into the park. Inside Hans found the heat even more intense with the sun beaming down on the parched lawns, the grass turned brown where sunbathers lay in bikinis worshipping Helios.

> "...Stay, stay until the hasting day has run
> But to the evensong;
> And having prayed together
> We will go with you along."

Alas, the daffodils were long since dead. But the rose-trees braved it all basking in the autumn sunshine.

Good year for the winegrowers too, Hans thought, taking the book from his briefcase, they

What Colette Didn't Know

will be very pleased with this sunshine. It was a poetry book Colette got from the library, and Hans had brought it with him, because for some days now he had devoted his thoughts to poetry. Maybe it's the weather, he suggested to himself, this prolonged summer that has whetted my appetite for verse. But he wasn't sure, he admitted, with the book now open on his knees. Allowing himself to submerge into the hypnotic world of poetry, Hans soon became oblivion of things and people around him, even forgetting to smoke.

The sun, moving westward invaded the shade, glaring onto the page and causing his eyes to burn. Hans looked up at the sun, then looked round him like someone waking out of a sleep. He closed the book and held it in his hands looking down at the ground. After some minutes, as if having regained consciousness, he straightened up and threw one leg over the other. He put the book down on the bench, stretched his arms high into the air, then rubbed his hands over his face and dropped his arms onto the bench.

A queer world we're living in, he said to himself, pondering over what he had just being reading, and musing about the effect poetry can have on a person. He lit a cigarette, yeah, even me

Mike Crowley

forgetting to smoke, he laughed, while wandering in the valley of verse.

And all that studying! All to what avail? The company invaded his thoughts. Thirty years working for the company. Working? Hans burst out laughing and quickly opened the book again, so that those around wouldn't think he was talking to himself, but that he was laughing at something funny in the book. You wouldn't call that work, Hans, would you,? he continued, trying to smother his laughing, now seriously becoming involved in a kind of cross-examination of his situation. No, Hans, work is something else, not what you were doing. He drew on his cigarette, his eyes focused on the open book, but he wasn't reading it. What you were doing wasn't work; at best a form of job creation. A waste of time. He put the book open face down on the bench, crushed the butt under his shoe and went and threw it into a nearby litter-bin. The sun had wandered on leaving him again in the shade.

You know, Hans, he said to himself, taking a seat again, you're finished with that company. He took the book, closed it and placed it on his lap holding it in one hand. And besides, you're glad to be finished with it. Idleness is indeed a great gift.

What Colette Didn't Know

Isn't it some feeling when you wake in the morning and know you can arrange your day doing whatever you want to do? Not having to say, I must do this or I must do that? Or, even worse still, having someone tell you what you have to do. You don't even remember their blasted names anymore. People you worked with for years, meeting them almost on a daily basis. Forgotten! Neuheimer. That ghost will probably follow me till I die, he laughed. For Hans, the old staff members were reduced to shadows. Their names deleted from his memory like computer data from a disk. He lit another cigarette. A change had come over him, he felt. He was no longer imprisoned in the agonizing mourning over the loss of his job. On the contrary, his new state of idleness challenged all what Hans had believed to be important in life. It caused him to laugh at himself, how he had wasted so many years of his life in a make-belief world.

The sun was gone down and the sunbathers gone home with only Hans and the empty benches left behind. Some pigeons and other small birds remained too, picking in the gravel. But they too, Hans thought, seemed willing to call it a day, and were just biding their time till bedtime.

Mike Crowley

Hans glanced at his watch. Well, he said to himself, putting the book into his briefcase, I suppose, I must be moving off too. But this time, walking over the gravelled path and out onto the street, Hans knew that he was no longer the same man he was when he had entered the park some hours before. This new feeling was a great feeling. It made him want to laugh at the whole world.

Chapter 15

It was St. Nicholas' Day, the day when children get presents if they have behaved well during the past year. On her way to work, Colette didn't notice the little men with a pipe, offered in every baker's shop on that day. But during the day, she found out all about it, and that Nikolaustag was one thing and Christmas another. What a nice custom, Colette laughed, listening while her colleaugues explained.

That afternoon, on her way home from work, Colette stopped over in town to do some shopping. Coming out of the U-Bahn station, she thought about Nikolaus, and decided to phone Hans and tell him she'd like to go and eat a pizza that evening with him, where could they meet? Before phoning however, Colette went into a baker's for a Nikolaus. A little surprise for Hans when he'd arrive home. She found the number on the display and put the mobile to her ear. Nothing doing! The mobile was dead. She tried a few times, but nothing happened. Strange, Colette thought, wondering and looking round with the mobile in her hand. Something's wrong, she thought, and noticed that other people were also acting, as if they were having problems with their mobiles. Not only me, she thought, as she stood watching them. They fiddled with the buttons, again put the mobile to their ear, but nothing seemed to happen. It was amusing to watch them, because it appeared, as if they just could not understand that something like this could happen. Colette put the mobile into her bag and took out her notebook. She had never before phoned the office number, because Hans told her, it would be better to use his mobile number when calling him. If he didn't answer, Colette would know that he was busy, probably in a meeting. Now she would have to ring the office number anyway, she told herself, as the mobile doesn't work. After waiting for some time at a public phone, while others phoned, all saying the same thing, that the mobile doesn't work, Colette finally dialled. Well, I'm not the only one then, she thought, as she stood listing to the dialling tone.

May I speak to Mr Konrad, please?

Sorry, a female voice said, I'm afraid Mr Konrad is no longer in the firm.

Oh!, you mean he's gone home already?

No, Mr Konrad left the firm the end of June.

Pardon me, but I'm talking about Mr Hans Konrad.

That's right. Like I just told you, he doesn't work here anymore.

Colette wanted to say something, but her mouth dried and she felt her throat tighten, the words, struggling to come out almost choking her. Dazed and confused, she hung up, but remained there standing, her hand still resting on the receiver, listening to the beeping reminding her not to forget her call card. Mechanically she took the card from the slot.

Are you finished phoning?, someone asked.

Yes!, yes!, she answered, startled, as if in a trance, and she moved off a few paces.

Mike Crowley

Hans doesn't work there anymore?... Since June? What Colette didn't know.

Colette walked off towards the escalator. She stopped in front of it, and changed her mind. Instead, she went and climbed the steps, pulling herself up step by step, holding onto the iron banister, to make sure she didn't stumble.

On reaching the shopping mile, she stood and gazed around her at the pedestrians that rushed past her. Left the company six months ago, she said to herself, staring into nowhere. She felt that what was taking place around her was like in a dream. What was gone wrong with her world so suddenly? It was no longer the world she knew only ten minutes before.

Dazed, she moved along the wet street, trying not to step on the pigeons that were dodging in and out under the people's legs, picking her way through the shoppers all caught up in the jolly spirit of the season, the brightly lighted shop windows, with the sounds of Christmas music and carols coming out of every corner, and the beggars sitting, huddled in corners holding out a tub for money. Idlers, Hans had called them. Too lazy to work. And himself? Six months idle.

What Colette Didn't Know

Colette wasn't feeling well. Nausea was setting in, an unsteady feeling in her legs, like someone that just got off a boat, after spending weeks at sea. Her world swayed.

In the midst of all this, the chimes of church bells mingled with the sweet smell of cinnamon, mulled wine, aromatic sweets and incense, that came from the Christmas stalls, where people crowded round buying presents and decorations for the festive season. A coffee is what I need, Colette told herself, looking around trying to orient herself in all her confusion.

Somehow that doesn't make sense. He gets up and goes out to work every morning. Colette went into a big store for a coffee. And still it's funny, Hans didn't tell me about it. Six months ago? Why, that was around June or July. Seated at a table near the window, Colette looked out over the city now shrouded in a kind of milky fog. But the coffee was good and it warmed her. She needed it too, badly, because the shock had chilled her to the bone. I wonder was he fired or did he go himself? Come to think of it now, Hans did say something about quitting work. But he never mentioned when. I need more time for writing, he said that time, and now that I'm turned fifty, I'll have to start thinking about myself. And, of course you, he added. But Hans couldn't have meant that, she thought, he had a good position and a good wage. Still hugging her cup, Colette gave up the idea of going out for a pizza that evening.

The fog outside had turned to darkness, but down below in the street the blinking lights of the Christmas decorations shone all the brighter. Colette got up and got herself another coffee. She was tired too of all that thinking. Returning to her seat, she was lucky it wasn't taken, she took a sip of her coffee... And then there were the letters, she went on. Hans never used to bother about the post. When there was post for him, Colette put it on the table where he always sat. In recent months though, Hans had the post collected before she got home. But where does he go every morning, if he doesn't go to work? How could he have put on a show like that over all these months? A woman, she thought, and Colette almost let the cup fall out of her hand. A woman!, Hans has a girlfriend. A chill ran down her back at the thought of it. The thundering rogue! No work, but time for his woman every day. She stood up and left, because she could stomach no more of it. She got the tram

What Colette Didn't Know

home. Later that evening she heard in the news, that the mobile system in and around the city had broken down, but that now things have been restored again.

When Hans came home, Colette confronted him with a question.

Where are you coming from at this hour?
Hans turned pale, looked at her and thought, it's the tone that makes the music. Up till now, it was quite clear, that when Hans arrived home in the evening, he came from work, where else should he be coming from,? So why now this question?

Why,? from work, Colette, why do you ask?
They stood facing each other, and Hans could see the rage gathering in Colette's face.

So, so. From work? Have you got a new job?
Almighty god, Hans thought, she's found it out, and he felt his mouth getting dry.

Well, Hans, she demanded, have you lost your tongue as well as your work?
Hans moistened his lips with his tongue as he started moving towards her.

Stay just right there where you are, Colette shouted, I want an answer to my question.
The answer you just gave me is a lie.

Mike Crowley

Hans, after moistening his lips again said, I'll explain everything, Colette, but could we go into the living-room and talk it over?

Hans wanted to explain to Colette the reason he had for not having told her. He wanted to tell her what happened the first day back to work after their honeymoon. How he found a letter on his desk without any previous hint that his job might be in jeopardy. It came as a shock and an insult that he, a long-time employee should be put out on the street just like that, a victim of accomplished facts. Could Colette not understand how insulted he must have been then? What, he wanted to ask her, what would she have done in such a case? But Colette didn't want to hear anything. She refused to listen to him. Instead she said, And what about me? Have you not insulted me by keeping it a secret? Keeping it all to yourself as if I didn't exist? With that she jumped up and ran into the bedroom. Hans followed and tried the door, but it was locked. He put his ear to the door and thought he heard sobbing, though he wasn't quite sure. Insulted, he thought, Colette is insulted. I was too, he thought, but I've grown accustomed to my situation. With his ear still glued to the door, Hans thought the crying had

What Colette Didn't Know

stopped. She's fallen asleep, he said to himself going back to the sofa. I'll sleep here tonight, he said to himself, taking off his shoes and socks. He put a cushion under his head, stretched out on the sofa and thought, pulling a rug over himself, no use making a scene.

Chapter 16

It was well into the afternoon when Hans left the house. He could in no way face Colette when she would arrive in from work. Surprising enough, that she had gone to work that morning, Hans thought, hurrying down the stairs. Outside on the street he stopped and hesitated as to whether or not he should go to his local. No, he decided, walking on, but stopping again to light a cigarette, I need a change of air. Better take the side streets into town, he suggested, that way I won't bump into Colette. Steer clear of the tram route.

At that time of year the afternoon quickly turned

to evening, but down town all the shops were lit up for Christmas. Just last weekend Colette and himself had wandered round the Christmas market, drinking Glühwein, mulled wine, looking at the stalls, commenting easily about all they saw and considering how they might spend Christmas. Maybe take a run down to Colmar. Hans, jolly and laughing reassuring Colette that, We'll surely work out some sort of surprise, our first Christmas together. Remember, Colette, you couldn't get time off last year. Colette laughed, slid her arm into his, and gave him a kiss on the cheek.

Hans took a seat at a vacant table. It was warm and smoky. Hans wasn't a regular there, but he often dropped in for a quick beer on his way home from work.

Where have you been all this time? the waitress inquired laughing, coming over to his table, It's a very long time since you were here. Hans smiled. He knew she was only half serious half joking.

Busy, he said, I was away for some weeks.

Ha!, ha!, she said, busy making money. Hans laughed.

The usual? she asked.

Hans lit a cigarette settling himself in his chair.

What Colette Didn't Know

He blew out the smoke and watched it float upwards mingling with the greyish haze hanging just above the shelves, where bottles of wine, rum, whiskey and several other spirits were on display. At times when the smoke got so intense that even hardened smokers couldn't stomach it, a waitress would open a very small window high up close to the ceiling. Passers-by, seeing the volume of smoke escaping from the pub, could be lead to believe that the place must be on fire. But the calm jolly faces of the people sitting inside would assure them that nothing was wrong; it was only smoke.

Zum Wohl!, the waitress said, Your health!, putting the glass on the table with a beer mat under it.

Thanks!, Hans said, looking after her. Then he focused his eyes on the yellow drink with the white crown, before putting it to his lips.

Men came in, drank a beer and were gone again. Others, intending to stay longer, took up position on high stools at the bar. They were regulars. Hans more or less knew them, because he had often seen them there. Work was over for today, and now they were settling down for a few drinks. On entering they exchanged some few words with those they knew, their eyes searching for a vacant seat. Outside the little light there was had faded into darkness, with only the shop lights glaring. It looked cold and the stream of people had thinned out to a trickle. Inside the atmosphere was jolly and Hans was feeling mellow. And a Korn too, please, Hans said, ordering yet another drink.

When the Korn came, he knocked it down in one go, and sent half the glass of beer down after it. Heidi Korn, he muttered, licking his lips. Ah!, girl, you got out of the way in time. You did indeed! But no blame on you. Just look at me... No future! Flexibility!, he muttered, putting the glass to his lips, the magic word! Hans raised his head and looked at the men seated at the bar. Never mind me, he thought, I'm only trying to sort things out. Nothing important, mind you, letting his head hang again. Flexibility!, be available at all times. Forget your thirty-eight hours a week. The company pays you, so dance to its music.

Hans stopped thinking. But you were all for it, Hans, weren't you? It helped you get a few feathers in your hat! Am I right? You knew damned well, Hans, he lolled away, that those old

What Colette Didn't Know

buggers you helped put out on the street, would never get work again. Unemployment didn't effect you, he continued, you thought you were sitting firm in the saddle. And all the time you didn't realize you were digging your own grave. Or as Hans put it, that he was in fact sawing the branch he himself was sitting on. You old fool, flexibility and lean management. And not even your friend Neuheimer could save you. And now there's Colette and the big row last night. What are you going to say to her tonight? Have you thought that one out?

He took a drink from his glass...Well, he started, had she been prepared to listen to me last night, it might be easier tonight. Nobody can say that I didn't want to tell Colette what happened. I knew damn well, I would have to own up to telling her sooner or later. But it was a problem. You don't just put a man out on the street like that. But Colette didn't want to hear it. I was always waiting for a solution. Sitting on a bench in a park, reading the newspaper in a café or even killing time at the airport, the matter worried me everywhere I went.

Thinking about it, Hans kept on turning over plans in his mind as to how best he could break the news to Colette. That one evening on the way home I wanted to buy flowers and when Colette would ask me how my day was, as she always did, I'd try to avoid giving her a straight answer. Then after supper, I'd say I had a little secret to tell her.

But we have no secrets between us, Hans, have we?
No, I told myself that time, that's not the right approach, Hans, it won't work.
Then there was that day, it was still summer, he was sitting in one of his hide-outs drawing pensively on his cigarette like someone trying to work out a solution to some problem or other. He looked about him, not looking at anything in particular. A man in a predicament. Only recently married, back from a wonderful honeymoon, sacked, and he couldn't find a way to tell his wife. It's all a dream, he thought, I've left the world and landed on some other planet. He was a man that was used to making decisions, but here he was now at a loss what to do.
I'll take the direct approach, he told himself one day, after considering the matter for weeks. He crushed the cigarette-end and tossed it into the litter-bin beside the bench where he was sitting.

What Colette Didn't Know

The direct approach, he repeated, settling himself in his seat, as if bracing himself for a conflict. What would that be? he asked, as if putting the question to someone. Waiting for an answer, Hans stretched his arms over the back of the bench, looked up at the sky and closed his eyes.

I'll go home now, he used to propose, and tell Colette I had a very bad day, but that doesn't matter anymore, because I'm fired. Colette will then look at me to see if I'm joking, but I'll notice the twinkle in her eyes darken. Fired, Colette, I'll repeat, the bastards threw me out on the street. Still uncertain, Colette will throw her arms round my neck and kiss me while the tears roll down my cheeks.

Hans stopped his monologue abruptly and lit a cigarette. I don't know, he said, and, after awhile, I don't know.

With decisions like "not tonight anyway," his plans as to how to break the news to Colette ended. And now, that the balloon has gone up, he thought, his trouble is how to face Colette for the second night.

Hans paid, emptied his glass, crumpled his cigarette-butt in the ashtray and left the pub after going for a piss.

Mike Crowley

Colette came home to an empty flat. She wasn't really sure if she had reckoned with or expected it like this. She was still too addled in her mind to sort it all out. Work and the colleagues had helped settle her nerves a little, and she even admitted to herself, that it must have been very hard for Hans, after all those years in the company, to be fired just like that. After making a coffee for herself, Colette set about preparing the evening meal.

When she had late shift, Hans always said, he'd look after himself. It was in fact no great trouble, because he always had lunch in the canteen. Imagine, Colette said to herself, Hans telling me all this and he almost six months out of work. When the food was ready, Colette put it into the oven at a low temperature till Hans arrived. She then went and got a French newspaper from her bag, that she brought with her from the office, and sunk into the sofa.

Burying herself in the newspaper, Colette soon forgot Hans, avidly reading everything there was in it about Paris. Having read through it she looked up and glanced at the clock, with what she read still dancing around in her head, and discovered that nearly two hours were gone. No sign of Hans, she said, folding the newspaper, I'm

What Colette Didn't Know

going to eat now, with or without him.

After her supper she sat watching TV, and after the news, she decided it was time for her to retire, she'd have to be up early for work. Where in the hell is Hans? she asked herself going into the bathroom, not a word from him the whole day. Her teeth brushed and ready for bed, Colette went into the bedroom, but she did not go straight to bed. Instead, she went to the dressing table and took out her diary. Sitting on the side of the bed, hot tears dropped onto the open page, when she read what she had written there only about six months before. "There are no secrets between Hans and myself. Hans tells me everything, especially about the office."

Somewhat inebriated, but nonetheless still in control, Hans sauntered off aimlessly through the night. No!, he wouldn't go home yet, he needed fresh air. He stopped to light a cigarette, then wandered on. The shops had long ago closed, but the windows were all brightly lighted. The streets were almost empty, but for a small group of men huddled together. Homeless men bedding down for the night in the archway of a large store. They were chatting, smoking and drinking beer from bottles. Is this how you're going to wind up? Hans asked himself, walking on. Flexibility, lean management. The devil take it!

The red-light district was ablaze with lights. Signs flashing outside every night club. Hans went into a pub, not a night club. He was surprised how quiet it was inside there, only a few men sitting at the bar drinking and chatting. Hans took a seat at a table and ordered a beer. He lit a cigarette adding to the already dense haze of smoke.
Hans knocked down the beer in one go. He was thirsty. Should he get a Korn? He had forgotten about it, even before he could make up his mind. No, things weren't going well. He called another drink. Now and then the blokes at the bar looked over at Hans muttering to himself. But it was quiet. Nice place for a drink. Terribly thirsty, Hans, he muttered, beckoning to the waitress for another beer. He lit a cigarette. Nice and snug, he said to the glass, glancing round at the tables. Wonder what Colette's doing? In bed, I suppose. He glanced at his watch. Getting late, Hans, he mumbled to himself. Yes, I'll have another, and a

What Colette Didn't Know

Korn, please, he said to the waitress standing at the table with his empty glass in her hand. When Hans had the Korn and beer inside him, he decided to call it a night. He'd go home.

He staggered out onto the street, the cold night air gripping him like a vice. The windows of the brothels on both sides of the street were dazzled in lights. Red, pink, orange. Pimps stood outside the doors of night clubs, and prostitutes went about their business, chatting up possible would-be clients. A woman came up to Hans and said, "Hallo sweety, how bout the two of us? Fifty for you, all in." Hans staggered on without giving her an answer. Further up the street he cupped his hands in a doorway and lit a cigarette. Then he pulled up the collar of his coat and started walking.

When the police arrived, Colette was fast asleep with the alarm clock set. She put out her hand from under the blankets and switched the alarm off, but the ringing went on. With her hand back under the warm blankets, she said, The door! it's the doorbell! She jumped up and ran into the hall. Hans locked out! Can't find his key, she thought, switching on the light and speaking into the intercom.

What Colette Didn't Know

  Going through his belongings, before returning to Paris, Colette found a last will and testament. An indication? Who knows?
As for the manuscript? Hans hadn't added a single word to it since their honeymoon.

ISBN 142510297-2